WOLF OF SHADOWS

SHIFTER REJECTED
BOOK THREE

AMELIA SHAW

CHAPTER

ONE

TALIA

I tugged my wolf shifter to the surface, ready for the fight I knew was coming. The ruckus I'd just heard could be something harmless, one of the witches' cats knocking stuff off my shelves maybe? Or a local kid playing a prank.

But according to all my instincts, that was doubtful. Very doubtful.

As I took another step down the hallway, my heart pounded inside my chest and my father's voice sounded in my head.

"Talia, when you grow up, you're going to have to fight 'em off with a stick."

Not a day had gone by without him uttering those words to me. He'd been right, but somehow, I doubted he'd meant 'fight' in the literal sense. Yet, here I was in my kitchen armed with a broken broom handle, prepared to battle it out with whomever had broken into the alpha's house.

Fight them off with a stick.

Yeah, thanks for that, Dad.

I could take care of myself in a fight. A fair fight. I had a sneaking

1

suspicion that it was more than a rogue wolf shifter who was guilty of breaking and entering in this instance.

"Show yourself." With my makeshift spear at the ready, I crept along the corridor toward my bedroom. "I know you're here. What are you waiting for? Come out."

Under normal circumstances, taunting a person who had no qualms about breaking into someone's home wouldn't be a good idea. But my circumstances were far from normal. I'd been rejected by my mate, kicked out of my pack, and abducted by an alpha who had given me a home–and fueled more than a few heated dreams, I had to admit.

And that was just in the past week.

The hits kept on coming, and I was sick of taking them lying down. I was finally ready to hit back. Maddox had learned that the hard way when he followed his father's orders and attacked Galen's pack the night before. I wasn't the same wolf that had been used, abused, and tossed away like yesterday's garbage by my former pack. They couldn't hurt me anymore.

My old alpha, the pack members who wanted me dead, and even Maddox had lost their hold over me when I'd realized how little they cared for me. They'd had no use for me once my father was dead and buried.

And to think I'd almost married Maddox.

In stark contrast, Galen's pack had taken me in and protected me when they should have cut me loose the minute they realized I wasn't the bargaining chip they thought I was.

I'd fought Maddox the night before and claimed a narrow victory. Still, a narrow win was still a win and I'd take it. Besting a wolf like Maddox had gone a long way in proving myself to Galen and his pack. I'd surprised them.

Hell, I'd even surprised myself.

I expected my ex to go home and lick his wounds. Not the physical ones he'd suffered during our fight–shifters healed too fast for that—but the psychological ones. He'd lost a fight to the girl he'd rejected and cast away. A burn like that needed more than aloe to heal.

My own injuries were all but gone. Just a few muscle kinks that could as easily be attributed to my afternoon make out session with Galen as they could an altercation with Maddox.

Still, if he wanted to square up for round two, I was ready.

"Maddox, I know it's you," I called out, assuming it had to be him, or one of his lackeys. Tired of the hide-and-seek nonsense, I tightened my grip on the wooden handle and stepped up to my bedroom door.

Max was bed-bound and resting in his room at the front of the house, still stricken with whatever illness plagued him. His spirit was strong, but his body—both man and wolf—had been weakened. He was vulnerable, unable to protect himself.

It fell to me to keep us both safe. But safe from what? I'd yet to see anyone. I'd heard the crashing noises of someone breaking in, but where were they?

I began to doubt the presumption that Maddox was behind the break in. If he, or one of his lackeys, was in my house, they would have made their presence known. Max and I were alone. The intruder had plenty of opportunities to attack, but they hadn't.

If it wasn't someone from my old pack, then who?

Or better yet, what?

I'd sensed a demon during the pack battle, felt its control over the wolves. It spurred on their thirst for blood and vengeance until the dirt was soaked in it. The dead and dying had littered the ground.

I was beginning to suspect a demon was behind this break-in attempt as well.

Maybe it wanted to test for weaknesses in our defense system and gauge how many wolves left in Galen's pack were willing and able to come to my aid.

Or maybe I'd already scared it off? That seemed unlikely though.

Back pressed against the wall, broom stick in hand, I took a deep breath and pushed open the door to my room. I thrust the jagged, broken end of the handle up and out.

I'd hoped to go on the offensive, turning the tables on the home invader, and catch them off guard but when I pushed open the door fully, no one was there.

Inside the room, the bed had been pulled from the wall and stripped of its sheets. The closet had been emptied, the contents scattered around the room. I assumed the upended bookcase had been the source of the crashing noise I'd heard.

Perhaps I was wrong in believing they were after me.

Were they looking for something in particular? I couldn't think of anything that would be of value to anyone. I'd been forced to leave a lot of my life behind when I was kicked out of my former pack and that included many of my material possessions.

If the intruder was a demon, they wouldn't be looking for money or jewelry. They were here for evil intent, and I intended to find out what that was.

Just as soon as I located the demon.

I hopscotched my way around the books scattered across the floor to the other side of my bedroom.

A creak came from the direction of the front door.

Fuck! Max was up that end of the house. *Get away from him.*

Broom handle tucked under my arm like a javelin, I rushed to the front of the house.

A demon waited for me in the kitchen. The yellow slitted eyes that blinked at me matched the gnarled and stained teeth in his crooked grin.

This one looked different to the other demons I'd met. More human-shaped, less flame. But even creepier somehow.

"Hello, Talia," the demon said, stretching out each syllable and wringing every ounce of sound possible from those two words.

Adrenaline zipped along my veins. My legs trembled with the need to run away.

But I couldn't run. Not with Max here, vulnerable. This pack took care of its own and if I wanted to be a part of that the pack community, I needed to do everything in my power to protect Galen's father.

Just like Galen would do if he was here. And what I wished someone had done for my father.

"Where's your alpha?" The demon wrapped his meaty fingers around the kitchen counter edge, splintering the marble beneath the force of his grip. "He went and left you all alone?"

"Who says I'm alone?" I snapped the broomstick in half over my knee and twirled the two pieces in my hand, mimicking a move I'd seen in one of those blockbuster action movies.

"The sick old man doesn't count." The demon ran his hand along the counter as he stepped closer toward the front door, then he turned around and came back again. The treads groaned under his weight, threatening to give way. "You're wasting your time playing nursemaid. I can smell the death on him from here. Let me save you the trouble."

"I'm surprised you can smell anything over your own stench and if you even think about touching him, I will kill you where you stand." I steeled my spine, held my ground, and prepared to make good on my threat.

"Oh, I'll do more than think about it, little wolf." The demon closed the distance between us. His hot breath was as rank as his body odor. "But I think I'll play with you first."

Anger unlike anything I'd ever felt before raised its ugly head inside me. This was not the day I would die. Nor would Max. Not on my watch.

"Oh, you want to play?" I swung the stick and landed the first blow with a crack to the side of his face, splitting his almost-human cheek wide open. "Let's play."

He pressed his hand against his cheek, eyes widening at sight of his own blood staining his fingertips. The demon shoved all four fingers in his mouth at once and suckled them clean.

"I like your spirit, little wolf." He slid his tongue under his lip and sucked his teeth. "I'm going to enjoy feasting upon it."

The demon reached for my arm. I whacked him as hard as I could with the piece of broom handle in my left hand.

"Foreplay." His grin sent chills down my spine. "A wolf after my own heart."

"Demons don't have hearts." I dodged right, out of the way of his left hook, and swung the stick to hit him again. And again.

My muscles, still a little sore from the night before, ached in protest of another round of abuse, but I refused to quit swinging the stick. I didn't care how big or bad this demon was. I would fight to the last breath.

Just like I had with Maddox.

"Talia," Max shouted from the bedroom. "Are you all right? Tal—"

He erupted into a fit of coughing. The illness wreaked havoc on his respiratory system, reducing his lung capacity and making it difficult for him to raise his voice.

"Talia?" he called again.

"I'm fine, Max," I yelled, sweat breaking out on my upper lip.

That was a lie. I knew it, and he knew it.

It didn't stop me from telling another one.

"I've got it all under control."

Things were far from under control. A demon was in the house uninvited.

This didn't feel like the work of my old pack. Maddox and his father had never outsourced their dirty work in the past. They preferred to handle their own business.

"What do you want? Who sent you?" I doubted the demon would answer my questions, but I had to ask.

These demons had been following me for weeks now. I needed to know who they were, in order to find out why.

The demon lunged forward, arms outstretched, ready to grab ahold of me and presumably drag me off to hell—or the person who controlled him. I leaned back, just out of reach. The tips of his blackened fingertips grazed my forearm.

He muttered something that sounded like Latin. I didn't know enough Latin—or any, for that matter—to be sure, but I had a terrible feeling whatever he said wasn't good.

He narrowed his slitted eyes and crooked his finger, motioning for me to make another move. A request I was all too happy to oblige. I let loose a flurry of blows, hitting any vulnerable or exposed part of his body.

A viscous black substance oozed from his wounds and splattered the walls and floor. The demon spat out more of the thick darkened blood and left an inky splotch by my foot. He wiped his mouth from corner to corner on the back of his hand, revealing a vicious smile.

"My turn." The demon grabbed the floor lamp in the corner, swung for the stars, and connected with my right side.

Searing pain exploded in my shoulder socket and raced down my arm. Electric pain all the way to my fingertips was followed by a horrible pins-and-needles sensation, then nothing.

My fingers unfurled their grip from around my makeshift weapon of their own accord. The half-broom handle fell from my hand and clattered against the floor.

The demon aimed for my left side and swung again, no doubt hoping to incapacitate me. I moved out of the way, and he missed.

Even though he had rendered my right arm useless, he could have done much worse given his strength and speed. He was a demon after all. *Strange.* He was holding back, wounding me but never issuing a killing blow. *Why?*

I wasn't going to be so generous.

With my left arm, I swung the stick at him. Each whack of my stick was harder than the last. I put everything I had into every hit, hoping to knock him out. With a quick twist of the wrist, I adjusted my grip on the one broom stick I had left, jagged side out, and lunged.

The makeshift dagger drove straight into his chest. Ugly black blood spewed out around the wound.

"I'm a demon, not a vampire." He locked his gaze with mine.

I staggered back, pressing my back against the wall. I panted hard.

The demon eased the broken handle out of his chest. If it was painful, his stone-cold expression gave nothing away.

Black blood waterfalled down his leathery chest, pooling at his feet before it soaked into the gray shag rug.

"Talia," the alpha called from his bedroom down the hallway, followed by more coughing.

"Not now, Max," I shouted behind clenched teeth.

The demon lunged at me. I dipped down into a squat to avoid taking another hit to my shoulder.

Laughter rumbled through the demon's chest like crackling thunder.

It was clear the demon was toying with me, and I wanted to know why. I also wanted to stay alive, and I wasn't sure those two things went hand in hand.

Death made interrogation difficult—for both of us—but not impossible thanks to the witches now living on the pack's land.

I called on my wolf and the inherent earth magic, fused into the genetic code of every shifter, that controlled our change.

It was past time for me to stop fucking around and take the demon down.

CHAPTER
TWO

TALIA

My wolf answered the call to arms in record time. The change came easier and faster than ever before. My muscles and bones shifted, and my skin and hair morphed into a thick, coarse coat with little pain.

Where I'd once stood as a woman, I was now a large gray wolf.

My lips curled back on a snarling growl, exposing sharp canine teeth designed for tearing into meat. A shiver ran down my spine, but I shook it out like I would water beaded on my coat.

My wolf loved to hunt, but even she was apprehensive about the taste of demon.

Hackles raised, I reared back on my haunches and lunged for his throat. The demon knocked me away with the ease of swatting a fly.

I hit the floor and slid toward the living room. I dug my claws into the hardwood floor, leaving four deep tracks and curls of the raw pine beneath the veneer in my wake as I grappled for purchase. I went after him again.

My teeth sank into his arm and the acrid, viscous blood coated my mouth, triggering my gag reflex. As expected, demon tasted like shit. Wolves are carnivorous of course, but I found out the hard way there was at least one meat we wouldn't eat.

I heard Galen's heartbeat, recognizing its strong and steady rhythm, before I caught his scent. The demon's stench wreaked havoc on my sense of smell.

"Hell no. Talia!" Galen's voice was shocked. A quick glance showed him standing in the entrance of the opened front door.

As I released the demon's arm and staggered back, shaking the disgusting blood from my mouth, Galen pressed his index and middle finger beneath my jaw and raised my head until I met his gaze. He nodded and ran his fingers through my coat—as if to reassure me that he was there, that he was real—before he shifted.

Galen's wolf was the most beautiful beast I'd ever seen and every inch of him was alpha. He attacked the demon with fang and claw, shredding flesh from bone.

I jumped into the fray after him.

With Galen on the attack as well as me, the demon seemed to sense his demise. He backed into the dark corner and attempted to make an escape into the shadows. Galen gave no quarter and charged after him. His jaw snapped shut like a trap on the demon's throat and with a single, vicious shake of his head, Galen ripped it out.

I shifted back to human form first, relief winging through my heart. He had appeared like a guardian angel and saved my life, and likely Max's, too.

Galen dropped the demon body to the ground, gagging and retching over the taste. I empathized with his position. Demon tasted worse than I'd ever thought possible. Like poisoned charred flesh.

I waited for him to shift back to human. When he did, the thank you I was planning stuck in my throat. Instead, shyness took me. I couldn't take my eyes off his beauty. He grinned as he surveyed my own nakedness, his gaze raking me from head to toe.

The heat of embarrassment filled me. I turned and raced down the hallway naked to grab a change of clothes. Bloody man. Even after saving my life, he could still make me blush as hot as Hades.

When I was finally covered up again, I popped into Max's room. He was still coughing, struggling to stay sitting up, his back against the headboard.

I hurried over to him.

"Everyone's safe," I said, helping him lower back down onto his pillows. "Just a little run in with a demon, but he's gone now."

"I know you said everything was fine, but I thought I should message Galen." Max tapped his cell phone nestled next to the TV remote beside him on the bed. "Just in case."

"Smart man. I can see why you've been alpha for so long." I tucked the old pair of sweatpants for Galen I was carrying under my arm, bent down, and pecked a kiss on his cheek. "I'm sure Galen will come see you in a minute to fill you in on all the gory details."

"I love story time." The warmth of Max's smile wasn't enough to chase away the sadness in his eyes. His mysterious illness ravaged his body like galloping consumption, yet his mind and spirit were still that of a strong alpha wolf.

He didn't need to say how much he wanted to be out of his bed and back in the action. It was written all over his face, in the crease between his brows, the lines around his eyes, and the determined set of his jaw.

"Go on, give Galen something to put on. The sooner he gets dressed, the sooner I get to hear the details." Max patted my hand and sent me on my way.

Halfway down the hallway, the pungent smell of sulfur hit me like a sucker punch to the sinuses. My eyes watered and my throat tightened, but it didn't account for the vertigo and dizziness.

I set my hand to the wall for stability and paused to regain my balance.

"Talia? What is it?" Galen's bare feet padded across the hard-wood floor.

He was close, but I couldn't open my eyes to look at him out of fear I'd fall.

"What's wrong?"

"Nothing. I'm okay. Fighting the demon took more out of me than I thought." I took a deep breath, forced my eyes open, and plastered a reassuring smile on my face, but there was no hiding my white-knuckled death grip on the wall. "I grabbed you a pair of sweats."

I knew exactly where all his clothes were since I was still sleeping in his room and he was crashing on the couch. I hadn't moved any of his things and was still living out of a suitcase.

"Thanks." Galen caught the sweats I chucked at him. "Are you sure you're okay?"

He mistook my still-frozen position in the hallway for being injured when in fact, the sight of his naked body had rendered me immobile.

"Yeah, I'm good." I licked my bottom lip and let the truth fall from my lips. "I'd be better if you left those off though."

Max's raspy laugh from his room behind me was the douse of cold water I needed.

"I think we should talk about what happened first." Galen's devilish smile was a promise of things to come and caused a ripple of desire to run along my veins.

At least I have something to look forward to.

He eased the loose cotton pants up and over muscular thighs and chiseled hips, covering the well-endowed part of his body that had snagged my attention. Then he pulled the drawstring waist band tight below his navel. It was almost like he was teasing me, the way he did it so slowly, and it was with difficulty that I lifted my gaze up to his face.

"Okay." My tongue felt thick in my mouth, making coherent speech difficult.

Galen stirred feelings within me that I'd never experienced before. Being with him, the way he looked at me, the way he touched me, left me questioning the years I'd invested in Maddox.

"Come here." Galen offered his hand for me to hold as I walked back down the hall. "We're going to sit on the couch and talk this out until we figure out what—"

He stopped short when we reached the living room. The place was a mess. Scorch marks on the sofa. Books thrown across the carpet. The coffee table lay on its side.

"How about the kitchen? I'll make some coffee." I led him down the short hallway that connected the foyer to the kitchen.

"I think I'm going to need something stronger than coffee." Galen brought my hand to his mouth and brushed his lips against my knuckles. Instant reaction between my thighs. One I tried hard to ignore. In the circumstances, it seemed inappropriate to lust after Galen when the house was trashed and demons were on the hunt.

He sucked in a breath as if he felt something too, and turned our entwined hands, exposing my wrist. "How did this happen?"

"How did what happen?" I rotated my arm for a better look at my wrist.

"That's a pretty nasty burn." Galen untangled our fingers and held my forearm with both hands. His brow furrowed and the corners of his mouth curved down while he examined the wound. "Does it hurt? We should see if one of the witches has a salve to put on that."

"I can't even feel it. Weird. I don't remember burning myself on anything." I stared at the blistered skin, watching it turn an angrier shade of red before my eyes.

The larger blisters engulfed the smaller ones, merging together until a bizarre symbol that resembled a hieroglyph took shape on my arm.

"Um, this is…" Fear held me in its icy grip as I remembered the demon touching me and quoting Latin, raising goosebumps over my skin. A chill raced down my spine. "This isn't good, is it?"

"We need to talk to Marguerite and the coven. Now." Galen spun me around, flattened his palm against the middle of my back, and nudged me toward the front door.

The walk outside and along the road was like an out of body experience. I knew my legs were moving. I could see the bend of my knees as I took a step, one foot shuffling in front of the other, but I couldn't feel the ground beneath me.

The coven to which Galen had granted sanctuary had set up an encampment on pack lands. He had allowed them to use some of the cabins, but they'd also built their own private tents. Unlike the witches who still lived outside the property lines, the few who sought shelter from the wolves were symptom free of the curse that drove everyone mad and these coven members on pack territory remained untouched by the demons.

Which was more than I could say for myself.

It was obvious the wound on my arm was not an ordinary burn. I hadn't done anything to cause the injury and my wrist had been blemish-free prior to the fight with the demon. I'd been so preoccupied with not dying at the time, but there was no denying it.

I'd been marked by a demon.

Galen called Marguerite on his cell as we marched toward the cabins. He instructed her to lower the wards around their homes, giving us safe passage through to meet her.

It was the first time he'd spoken since we left my house. He explained the new lockdown procedures and intensified wards that had been put in place whenever there was an immediate threat to pack or property.

I wasn't an initiated member of his pack, and there were a handful of vocal wolves that made their opinions on the matter of my presence well known. But over the course of the short time I'd been here, Galen had treated me better than my own pack.

It was the most I'd belonged in my life.

Even when I'd been betrothed to Maddox, there had always been something missing, like I was the last piece to the wrong puzzle. All that had changed after Galen, which seemed crazy when I considered the circumstance of how we'd met.

Or maybe I was just crazy.

My life had been in a free fall with no end in sight for weeks now. A nervous breakdown seemed totally within the realm of possibilities after what I'd been through. How else could I explain my feelings for Galen and his father, or the rest of the pack, for that matter?

"Sarah is around. She's going to try and help us," Galen explained.

"Oh, great." I liked Sarah. She was younger than most of the other witches, and had a nice nature.

Galen and I continued down the main road of the pack lands toward the south end where the witches were housed. Sarah waited outside one of the bachelor cabins that had been sectioned off for the coven.

Her long red hair was twisted up into a bun on the top of her head. She wore a black silk robe over matching pajamas, the fabric a stark contrast to her pale skin.

Sarah hurried down the steps of the cabin and stepped in front of one of the pop-up tents some of the witches had set up in the front yard. They'd complained about the size of the housing and worked some of their magic to add to the accommodations.

The tent looked far too small for one grown person, let alone the three of us, but on the inside, it was glamping to the max and large enough for a party of twelve. I'd experienced their expanding magic several times and it never ceased to amaze me.

Sarah unzipped the opening and pulled back the flap, holding it open while Galen and I crawled through.

"This never gets old." I spun a slow circle in the entranceway, marveling at the details within the spell she'd crafted. She had everything a witch could want, from couch to cauldron to kitchen sink. "Can you spell the alpha's house? I'd love a bedroom so I don't need to steal Galen's anymore."

"Of course, I can." Sarah grinned. "But I'm not sure how the alpha will feel about that. Or Galen."

I slanted a look at Galen, who simply raised a brow at me.

"You're right." I focused on the idea of the alpha, not the sexy man standing in front of me. "I'd better ask Max first."

It wasn't my house, so I really shouldn't have said anything.

She locked her fingers together, turned her palms out, and raised her arms above her head, sighing as she stretched. "So, Galen didn't rush you over here to discuss renovations. What's the emergency?"

Fear and shame drove me to clamp my hand over my wrist, hiding the mark seared into my flesh.

"It's not going to go away on its own, Talia. She needs to see it." Galen pried my fingers from around my wrist and lifted my arm up for examination.

"Holy shit." Sarah's wide-eyed expression did nothing to quell my fears. "That's a demon mark."

"Yeah, we kind of figured that part out on our own," Galen grumbled.

I had no idea what it meant for the future. Was it, like... a homing beacon? A tracker? Just a weird burn I'd have to deal with forever?

No-one seemed to know, or they weren't telling me. Either way, I wanted it gone.

"Can you..." I stumbled over my words, afraid to ask the question or hear the answer. "Can you remove it?"

"Of course, I can." With her finger, she traced the outline of the demon mark burned into my skin. "But it'll cost you."

I tugged my arm free of her grip and considered how much money I had left in my cash stash. Enough... maybe.

"I'll pay for it." Galen draped his arm over my shoulder and tucked me against his side, holding me tight. "Whatever it costs."

"You sure, sugar daddy? This one's expensive." I felt Galen stiffen at the same time as me at the offensive term. She raised her hands, palms out, in a placating gesture and backed up a step. "Sorry, I didn't mean sugar daddy. I meant pack daddy... Alpha, that's what I meant. Sorry, this is what happens when I have too many energy elixirs.”

“How much is it going to cost, really?” I was more than a little concerned at the idea of being indebted to Galen, for what I feared would be a substantial amount of money, and how I would pay him back.

“It doesn’t matter how much,” Sarah said. She seemed to sense my apprehension over the looming debt. “He can’t pay it.”

“What do you mean, I can’t pay it?” Galen scoffed, reaching for his wallet. “I said, whatever the cost, and I meant it.”

“Trust me, if I could take your money, I would.” She turned her attention back to me, an unspoken apology in her eyes. “But the cost is Talia’s. She has to pay it, or the spell won’t work.”

In other words, I was screwed and on a fast track to hell.

CHAPTER

THREE

GALEN

Things went from bad to worse in a hurry. Talia hadn't shared the details of her financial situation, but I knew it wasn't good. She'd barely had time to establish a new life outside of her pack before I snatched her away from it.

And I'd ruined her life for nothing.

It was becoming a pattern. First with my girlfriend Jessie, and now with Talia. It looked like I wouldn't be able to save her either.

Fuck.

I should have done my homework. If I had, I would have known she wasn't engaged to the alpha's son, that she'd been tossed out of her pack, and taking her would be a waste of time.

Except, that wasn't true.

Nothing about Talia was a waste of time. I couldn't imagine a better way to spend my time than getting to know the strong, resourceful woman who'd chipped away at my armor and somehow managed to expose my heart.

"Well, I guess I belong to a demon." Talia slipped out from under my arm and flopped on the couch with an exasperated sigh. "What do you suppose slaves wear in hell? Uniforms? Jumpsuits? Or those coverall-looking things?"

"Oh, don't be so dramatic." Sarah waved off Talia's very valid fears and strolled over to a bookshelf on the far side of the tent. Her fingers danced along the book spines until she found the tome she was after. She plucked it off the shelf with a flourish.

"Easy for you to say. You're not the one shackled for all eternity to a demon." Talia hid her face behind a throw pillow and I suspected she was trying not to cry.

Her pain hit me like an arrow to my heart. I would have given anything to make it my own, but according to the witch, there was nothing I could do to save Talia. I was helpless, hopeless.

Again.

"First, we don't even know if that's what the mark means." Sarah opened the book, licked her index finger, and flipped through the pages until she found the right spell. "And second, the spell doesn't require money. It requires a sacrifice."

"A sacrifice?" My experience with witches was limited, but from what I'd gleaned of their craft in the time they'd been on pack lands, the word sacrifice could mean anything from blood to sweat, to tears.

Or all the above.

"A few drops of blood." She leaned into the book, squinting as she read the words scrawled across the rag paper page of the old tome. She glanced up from the spell book, her eyes wide. "Or a pint."

"A pint?" Talia shot upright and dropped the decorative pillow in her lap. "A pint of *my blood*?"

"It could be a cup." Sarah's gaze flitted from the spell, to Talia, then me. "I think it's a cup. The ink is smudged and faded. It's a little hard to make out, but if Talia makes a blood sacrifice, the spell should work."

"Should?" Talia said, sounding as frazzled as she looked.

I didn't blame her. The demons were responsible for the curse that drove the witches mad and led to hundreds of casualties. Every death, including those of innocent civilians caught in the crossfire, could be laid at their feet.

And now Talia was connected to one of them through the mark on her wrist.

"They call it practicing witchcraft for a reason." The witch shrugged, as she bustled around to gather the other ingredients for the spell.

Despite her casual attitude, the slight tremor in her hands when she pinched leaves from a dried bundle of herbs and tossed them into a pot gave her away. Talia was her friend, and I had no doubt Sarah cared about her.

So did I. Which was why the spell had to work.

I sat down on the empty couch cushion beside Talia. I cupped her face in my hands and brushed my thumbs across her cheeks, erasing the tracks of the tears she'd shed behind the pillow.

"Talia, look at me." I waited until she fixed her soul-piercing violet-blue eyes on me, before continuing what I hoped would be a motivational speech. For the both of us. "She's just messing around, all right? She can do this. *You* can do this. Hell, you lost more blood kicking Maddox's ass. You held your own in a fight with a demon. This is nothing."

That earned me the first genuine smile I'd seen on her face since the demon attack at my dad's house.

"You're right. I'm sorry. I don't know what's gotten into me. I just feel off my game." She tilted her head and pressed a kiss against my palm. "I guess the demon mark has me a little freaked out."

"Oh, my goddess." Sarah pressed her hand against her chest and expelled a deep breath of air. "Me too."

"Not helping." I closed my eyes and pinched the bridge of my nose, shaking my head.

Talia laughed and the sound was music to my ears. She deserved to be happy after all the shit she'd been through; was still going through. I found myself wanting more and more to be the person that made her feel that way.

"Okay, I'm ready. Let's do this before I chicken out." She leaned in close, her voice barely above a whisper when she spoke. "This may come as a shock to you, but I'm not big on the sight of blood. Especially my own."

"A lover not a fighter, huh?" I teased, taking her hand in mine. I couldn't get enough of Talia and seized every opportunity to touch her.

I knew better than to get involved. I knew how it would end— with a broken heart. Mine. I'd cobbled it back together after my last doomed relationship. I didn't think I had it in me to go through that again.

But the way she looked at me, like I'd hung the moon, made me want to try.

"Truth be told, I hadn't had a lot of experience in either area until recently. I mean, besides Maddox." One corner of her mouth curved up in a lopsided grin. "Who, coincidentally, fell into both categories."

The thought of her with someone else—with Maddox— ignited a jealous streak in me that I never knew existed. Not even with my ex, and I had been head-over-heels for that woman.

Or at least I'd thought I was.

The way I felt about Talia had me questioning every relationship I'd ever had and whether I knew what love truly was before I met her. It pained me to admit it, but I wasn't sure that I did. The one thing I knew for sure was that Maddox didn't deserve her or the years she'd given him.

What I wouldn't give for a fraction of that time with her, moments curled up beside her in bed.

This woman would be my undoing.

Sarah finished her preparations and handed Talia an athame. The short Damascus steel blade, used for rituals and ceremonies, was etched with runes down the center and razor sharp.

"Will you do it?" Talia set the dagger in my lap. "I don't think I can do it myself. Look at my hands. They're shaking."

Her nerves were getting the better of her. Talia had a lot riding on her friend's spell. So did I. If something happened to her, if she was hurt or the demon claimed her, I'd never forgive myself. I couldn't lose her.

Especially to a demon.

We didn't know what the symbol meant, but it wa pretty obvious it wasn't anything good.

Demon marks weren't just handed out by hell-spawn. They were a form of currency among demons and a barter system with humans —and werewolves, apparently. Demons used them to seal a deal, a piece of your soul traded for a wish from the destitute and desperate. The mark was physical proof of a contract made, carried through life and claimed upon death.

But Talia had made no such deal.

The demon had branded her with its mark on her wrist, claiming a piece of her soul without Talia getting anything in return. That shouldn't have been possible.

I picked up the blade and turned it over in my hand, taking care not to nick myself with the sharp edge, contaminating the blood sacrifice with my DNA. The ornate handle, encrusted with opal and other semi-precious stones, felt lighter than I expected. In fact, the weapon was perfectly balanced.

Talia held my gaze and with a nod of assurance that she was ready, held out her hand. I supported her hand with my left and traced the line running across her palm with the blade of the athame.

Bright crimson blood welled to the surface and puddled in the center of her cupped hand. Sarah rushed over with a silver chalice to collect the sacrifice. Talia lifted her hand from mine and squeezed it into a fist over the goblet, pumping her fingers to increase the flow.

"Is that enough?" Talia looked a little green and I worried she might pass out.

"Let me see." Sarah peered around Talia's bloody hand into the cup. "That's plenty. Here, this will help stem the flow of blood and speed up the healing process."

She removed the cup from under Talia's hand, exchanging it for a bandage she grabbed from the side table, a wound dressing slathered with a sweet-smelling poultice. She wrapped the bandage tight, tucking the loose end into one of the folds and turned Talia's hand over to examine her work.

Satisfied with the dressing, she gave Talia her hand back and took the silver chalice filled with her blood to a small countertop cauldron with a firebox underneath. She blew on the smoldering embers, bringing them back to life as she stoked the fire. The sap in the pine crackled and popped, fueling the fire as it oozed out of the wood pulp.

Sarah checked the spell book, muttering to herself as she grabbed various jars and added a pinch of this and a dash of that. She finished the concoction with the dried herbs she'd already prepared and spoke the words needed to invoke the spell.

"Drink this. All of it." She thrust the goblet into Talia's hand. "Bottoms up."

"Why does it smell like the landfill baked under the midday sun on the hottest day of summer?" Talia gagged when she brought the steaming brown potion to her mouth but tipped the cup back and choked down the liquid. "Blech, that was so gross. Now what?"

"Now we wait." Sarah reached over and rotated Talia's arm until the demon mark was visible. "The mark should disappear any moment now."

I ticked off the seconds in my mind, knots forming in my stomach with each one that passed. Nothing happened. The mark on Talia's arm looked as sore and irritated as it had before she drank the potion.

"What does this mean? Why isn't it working?" Talia cradled her marked arm to her chest and tucked in her chin, her shoulders bobbing as she fought back tears.

The spell was an utter failure. That was what it meant. It didn't take witchcraft to figure that out.

"I... I don't know." Sarah sat on the edge of the couch cushion, pulled Talia into her arms, and rocked her back and forth. "I'm so sorry, Talia. I followed the spell's instructions to the letter. I don't understand what went wrong."

"What am I supposed to do now? Fight off every demon that tries to take me?" Talia shifted in her friend's arms and looked to me for answers.

I gave her the only one I had: "Yes. But you won't do it alone. I'll be with you, as will the pack."

My wolf paced behind my rib cage, ready to burst free at any moment. He wanted to hunt down whoever summoned the demon and deliver his own special brand of justice. Pack justice. As alpha, it was my responsibility to enforce the rule of law. I was the judge, jury, and executioner.

I couldn't have agreed more. When we found them, and I had no doubt that we would, they would pay in spades for what they did to Talia.

"I can ask the other members of my coven. If there's another spell that will work, the high priestess will know it." Sarah used the cuff of her sleeve to wipe Talia's tears and brushed the stray hairs out of her eyes.

"I'm calling a pack meeting." I stood up, pulled my phone out of my jeans pocket, and paced the floor while dialing David's number. He answered on the first ring. "Hey, get everyone together to the meeting hall. We need to talk, all of us, including the witches. I'm at Sarah's place. We'll bring the coven and meet you there."

The demons had invaded the wrong town and fucked with the wrong pack.

It was high time somebody taught them a lesson. It was up to my pack and me to do it. School was in session, and I was the teacher.

CHAPTER

FOUR

TALIA

The meeting hall wasn't large enough for all the pack members plus a full coven of witches, forcing Galen to hold the meeting outdoors. I shivered as a cold wind wrapped around my bare arms.

Galen offered me a sweatshirt he'd stowed in the back of his Jeep, and I nestled into the added warmth of another layer—and Galen's comforting scent permeating the heavy cotton fabric.

The sweatshirt hung down at my knees like a sack dress, drowning my small frame. I rolled the sleeves at the cuffs, leaving enough material to cover the demon mark on the inside of my wrist. Then I wedged my way to the front of the crowd that had gathered around Galen who was busy thanking everyone for coming on such short notice.

"I've asked you all here tonight to discuss the problems with the demons in our town. They're testing us, coming onto pack land, and tonight they attacked someone under my protection." Galen left out my name—and the demonic brand seared into my flesh—but everyone seemed to know who he was talking about.

I felt the weighted gaze of his pack members bearing down on

29

me and was grateful he decided not to make the demon mark public knowledge until we knew what it meant or what it would do.

While most of the pack had accepted me, there were still outliers wary of a castaway from a rival pack.

Not that I blamed them.

After my former pack attacked them and the casualties suffered under the orders of Maddox and his father, I wouldn't trust anyone from my pack either.

In fact, I didn't.

Galen's pack was the polar opposite of the one I'd been raised in. This was a community where people supported each other and worked together. I wanted more than anything to be a permanent part of it. I had hoped to prove myself and earn a place among them.

That was before I was demon marked.

My world had been turned upside down. Again. I had no clue if the demon would kill me or claim me. Both of those scenarios were horrible but being claimed by a demon scared me more than anything. There had to be a way to remove the mark. I just needed more time to figure it out.

But time wasn't on my side.

It seemed determined to work against me. The demons in town grew bolder. Maddox and his father were hell bent on seizing control of the whole territory and usurping Galen. I wanted justice for my father's murder.

And the town residents were caught in the crossfire.

The universe threw everything it had at me all at once and I struggled to keep up. I thought the public humiliation of a broken engagement and being kicked out of my pack was the worst thing that could happen to me.

How naïve could one person be?

I saw things clearly for the first time in my life. Maddox had done me a huge favor without even realizing it when he'd ended our relationship. I'd thought we loved each other, but I couldn't have been more wrong. Being alone was better than being trapped in an unhappy relationship.

The alpha of my pack had murdered my father. If he hadn't cast me out, justice would never be served. Not without a challenge. But outside of the pack, vengeance was mine.

And then there was Galen.

If I'd been engaged to Maddox and an active member in my old pack, there wouldn't have been a place for him in my heart.

And he'd taken up residence there in such a huge way that I now couldn't imagine my life without him in it.

Galen wrapped up the *why* of the meeting and moved on to the *what*—as in what he planned to do about the current demon situation.

"That's Marguerite, the high priestess, over there." Sarah had to elbow her way through the crowd to join me in the front row. She pointed to an older woman with silver hair and piercing blue eyes. "When the meeting's over, we'll ask her about... you know, your little problem."

Werewolves had excellent hearing, so I appreciated her discretion, but my problem was far from little.

It was a huge problem that left me feeling anxious and overwhelmed. Still, I was grateful to have a friend who stuck by my side and wanted to help.

We listened to Galen talk about the enhanced perimeter wards the witches agreed to install, along with their offer to upgrade the ones already in place. His decision to give them pack protection and allow them into pack lands had forged a powerful alliance with the coven.

It was an equal partnership and that meant the wolves wouldn't be able to rely solely on the coven's magic for protection. They needed to bring something to the table as well.

Which brought Galen to his second point in the meeting, one that grabbed my attention and refused to let go.

Watches were to be added to the regular security protocols in place. His beta would assign each wolf a partner. The pair would then be given a four-hour shift patrolling the borders of the pack land and alerting Galen or his beta of any demon sightings.

Under no circumstances were they to risk the wards and engage with the demons unless the latter crossed the property line and entered pack lands.

I wanted to help protect the pack and planned to volunteer for a watch as soon as the meeting was over and we'd spoken to the high priestess about my mark.

It was a chance for me to return the favor to Galen's pack for taking me in and to prove to the few skeptics that remained that they were wrong about me.

Two wolves, one stone. So to speak.

"I'm going to see if I can get Marguerite's attention, let her know we need her help, before she takes off to work on the wards." Sarah pulled me into a hug, squeezed tighter than normal, and whispered in my ear. "You'll be okay by yourself, right?"

"Of course. I'm a werewolf, remember? I'm never really alone." I swept away her worries with a much-needed laugh and squeezed her back.

The oversized sleeve of Galen's hoodie slid up my arm, exposing my wrist. I yanked the sleeve back down, clutching the cuff in my hand to ensure the mark stayed out of sight. To my relief, no one seemed to notice.

That was a close call. If someone saw the demon's mark, they might have reason to question Galen's leadership and loyalty to the pack for withholding information that could affect everyone.

That was something the members of my old pack would have done. Not out of concern for the pack, but as a power play. Anything to gain the advantage and jockey for a better position in the pack.

Galen's wolves seemed different, less interested in individual power and more concerned with what was best for the pack as a whole—the way it was supposed to be.

Still, I didn't want to do anything to jeopardize Galen's position or cause more friction within the pack than I already had. It was a close call, and I needed something better than a baggy sweatshirt to hide the mark.

Before someone noticed and figured out what it was.

"Hey, Talia," a familiar voice said from behind me.

I glanced over my shoulder, surprised to find the newest member of Galen's pack looming there.

"Darius. Hi." I tilted my head back to meet his gaze and offered a meager smile. "I'm sorry, I didn't realize you were standing right behind me this whole time."

The odd thing was, he hadn't been there the whole time. Darius stood out in a crowd. I would have remembered nudging past him to get to the front and there was no way I overlooked him when scanning the crowd after exposing the mark on my wrist.

He must have seen me and made the effort to work his way through the crowd to reach me. But to what purpose?

Darius's sudden appearance was unnerving, but more than likely I was being paranoid. I'd felt off kilter ever since the demon attack and that, combined with everything that happened in the last week, made me suspicious.

I'd been through two break-ups, one with a fiancé and one with a pack, an abduction, a whirlwind whiplash rebound, and a demon mark.

On second thought, maybe a little caution was warranted.

"Listen, I wanted to talk to you about... you know..." His gaze flicked down to my wrist before he stepped to the side, invading my personal space. He draped his arm around my shoulders. "In private."

Goosebumps prickled my skin and red flags popped up, waving erratically, in my mind.

Danger. Danger. Danger.

How had he seen me, *and the mark on my arm*, when I hadn't seen him anywhere in the people gathered for the pack meeting?

I needed that question answered. Against my better judgment, I let him steer me to a secluded spot near a copse of trees about a football field's length away from the safety and security of the crowded meeting area.

So much for caution.

"Galen left that out of the announcements." He hooked his finger on the cuff of my sleeve and hiked it up my arm, studying the mark. "You should be more careful. Someone other than me might have seen it and that could cause problems for the alpha."

The way he emphasized the latter made me wonder if he wasn't the one who would eventually cause problems for Galen.

"We weren't planning to keep it secret forever." I shifted on my feet. The impulse to bolt in the direction of the crowd increased the longer his finger lingered on my wrist. "It happened a couple of hours ago and we were hoping to find out what the symbol means before we said anything."

"You don't strike me as someone who'd make a deal with a demon." Darius encircled my wrist with his hand and brushed his thumb back and forth over the burn which was still sensitive to the touch. "How'd you get it?"

I wasn't used to having a wound that didn't heal and winced when he traced the blistered skin. A smile appeared then immediately disappeared from his face before it had the chance to fully form, as if he found pleasure in pain but didn't want me to know about that particular kink.

"There wasn't a deal, because I didn't make one." I bit down on the inside of my cheek hard enough to draw blood and tugged my arm free of his grip.

The metallic taste coated my tongue and provided a much-needed distraction from the sting of the burn.

"Demon marks don't just appear out of thin air." Darius narrowed his eyes, a deep line forming between his pinched brows, and crossed his arms over his chest. "Something must have happened."

"A demon showed up in my house and attacked me." I shook my

arm, encouraging the sleeve to slide back down, and bunched the rolled cuff in my fist. "I'm not sure when or how, but it marked me while I was fighting it off."

"*You* fought off a demon?" Darius looked me up and down. His gaze lingered on my breasts, giving me an unexpected reason to be grateful for the baggy sweatshirt.

"I held my own." I sidestepped to my right for a better view and looked past him to Galen and the small crowd of pack members surrounding him. "And then Galen showed up and finished him off."

"Galen." Darius said his alpha's name through gritted teeth, muscles twitching as he clenched his jaw. "I'm glad he was there to save the day."

The flat tone of his voice and flicker of anger in his eyes said otherwise.

But it wasn't violence toward Galen that I sensed from Darius. His anger seemed to be projected inward, not out. As if he was upset that he wasn't the one who had shown up at my house when the demon attacked.

I neither expected nor wanted jealousy from Darius, but it was better than greed. I'd half expected blackmail to be the reason he asked to speak to me alone.

The need to get back to Galen and Sarah outweighed the need to know how Darius had seen my mark.

I should have waited for Galen to finish the meeting and sought his advice on how to handle the situation with Darius instead of running off with him.

In the short time I'd known Galen, I'd leaned on him quite a bit. Probably more than I should have. He had enough on his plate as it was. I'd hoped to handle Darius myself and not add to it.

As usual, things didn't go according to plan.

It was time I made my exit.

"Listen, I appreciate the advice about the mark. I'll be more careful and keep it covered. I'm supposed to grab a bite with Sarah.

So, I should really get back." I stepped out of Darius's reach, relieved he didn't get physical when I walked away.

"I can help you." Darius jogged a few steps to close the distance I'd put between us. "With your mark, I mean. That's what I wanted to tell you. I think I can heal it."

How would a werewolf know how to heal a demon mark? I recalled the adage about curiosity and the cat and decided not to stick around to find out.

"Sarah is already working on something for me. She's gone to a lot of trouble to help me, so... But hey, if that doesn't work, we could try your way."

"She's a talented witch but a demon mark is beyond her abilities." Darius matched my pace stride for stride. "I just want to help you."

Something about his eagerness raised my hackles. My wolf stirred from her restorative nap after the fight with the demon and stalked forward until I felt the weight of her presence in my chest.

She was done talking and ready to fight our way out of the conversation.

CHAPTER

FIVE

GALEN

The meeting with the witches went off without a hitch. The coven wasted no time reinforcing the existing perimeter wards and Marguerite assured me that she would see to the new wards herself.

A few members of the pack were still leery of the witches living on pack lands, but the demons had grown bolder, and I was grateful for new allies.

Markus and I reviewed the security protocol one last time before we paired people up and assigned them a shift to be on watch.

It was all hands on deck until we stopped whoever was behind the demon attacks.

I checked two out of three items off the emergency to-do list. The last item on my list was for Talia to show Marguerite the demon mark and get the high priestess's opinion on how to remove it.

It looked like Sarah had things well in hand as far as the magical wards were concerned. She and Marguerite had their heads together and were deep in conversation.

Except, as I looked around, I didn't see Talia anywhere.

I thought she would have stayed with the coven while I wrapped up pack business but when I asked the witches, none of them had seen her. Marguerite agreed to examine the demon mark to see what if anything could be done.

But that required Talia and she was M.I.A.

A few witches offered divination services to help me locate her, but I didn't need incense and a crystal ball to find Talia.

Not when my wolf could pick up her scent and follow her trail.

I backtracked to the last place I'd seen her and sniffed out the different scents in the air until I found the one unique to Talia—orange blossoms and sunshine. The strength of her scent trail ebbed and flowed, almost disappearing when I reached the spot where she had stood during the meeting.

There were too many witches and wolves in one place, muddying the trail. I closed my eyes, inhaling a deep breath through my nose, and let my wolf go to work.

There.

It was faint, but it was enough. I followed her scent away from where the crowd was gathered to a more isolated area of the property. The smell of orange blossom intensified, but there was something else too.

Something not Talia.

Something male that put my wolf on edge. Neither of us were thrilled with Talia being alone with another guy. Jealousy reared its ugly head, making my fists tighten.

I recognized the other scent. Darius.

What's she doing with him?

There was something *off* about the newest member of our pack. I couldn't put my finger on what it was, but the more time I spent around him the more worried I became.

The decision to bring him into the pack was on me and I hoped I hadn't made a mistake.

With demon attacks and a curse on the witches, we needed as many wolves as we could get. I hadn't vetted him the way I normally would a new member. It was a rash decision made out of necessity.

One I hoped didn't come back to bite me in the ass.

I caught a glimpse of Talia near a small grove of evergreen trees, a secluded spot perfect for an intimate conversation.

Or something more.

Wolves were skilled hunters, stalking their prey before they attacked. My wolf and I were no exception. I treaded lightly, each step precise and without a sound.

Darius came into view, his fingers curled around her wrist and a possessive streak in his eyes. It seemed he'd taken an interest in Talia as well. My wolf never doubted our prowess and welcomed the competition.

I wished I shared my wolf's confidence and had to stifle a growl at the sight of another man touching her—regardless of whether or not the touch turned out to be innocent.

When it came to pack business, I had the courage and determination needed to lead. The same could not be said for relationships.

Not after Jessie.

Her death broke me. I'd pieced myself back together for the sake of the pack and focused all my energy on our community, but the personal scars were still there.

I was damaged goods.

Talia was a salve to my tattered soul. I caught glimpses of a future I thought I'd lost whenever we were together, but if I examined it too hard or looked too long, it disappeared. As much as I wanted to, I couldn't open my heart enough to commit.

Her wolf called to mine in a way I'd never felt before, and it scared the hell out of me.

Talia seemed to have all the confidence I lacked and knew what she wanted. Or at least, she knew what she didn't want.

And judging by her body language, the only kiss lover-boy was going to get from her was a fist across his lips.

I shouldn't have doubted her.

"There you are." I kept my pace and my tone casual, closing the distance between us as if I were out for a moonlight stroll. "I was looking for you. Figured you'd need a ride home."

It wasn't the night for a challenge. Not after a demon had attacked Talia. There wasn't any room left on my plate for more problems. When this was all over, if Darius wanted to throw down a challenge over Talia, I would be more than happy to accept.

In the meantime, her safety, and the safety of everyone under my protection, was my number one priority.

"Well, considering you drove me." Talia unfurled her closed fist and stepped away from Darius, joining me at my side. "Darius kept me company while you were finishing up."

I'd spent enough time with her to pick up on subtle nuances when she talked. There was more to the story—no surprise there—and I'd hear the rest of it as soon as we were alone.

"Galen." From Darius's curt nod and clipped one word greeting, I assumed he wasn't all that pleased to see his alpha.

I filed that away for later. *One problem at a time.*

"So, you're ready? Everything's all wrapped up?" Talia seemed eager to get away from Darius and hurried toward me.

"Think about what I said, Talia," Darius called after her, but he made the right choice and let her walk away. "I'm here to help."

"I appreciate it. If things don't work out, you'll be the first to know." Talia barreled past me in the direction of my truck and never looked back.

Darius took off in the opposite direction without as much as a goodbye. It was a blatant show of disrespect to his alpha, but under the circumstances I was forced to pick my battles.

And I was all too familiar with needing space to lick love's wounds. I'd won this battle. Talia was heading home with me, so I decided to cut him some slack.

I waited until we reached my truck and the privacy of its extended cab before I asked, "What the hell was that all about? Spill."

"Somehow, he saw the burn on my arm." Talia rubbed the spot

on her wrist where the demon had left his mark. "The crazy thing is I don't even know how. He wasn't there when I jockeyed my way to the front of the crowd. Or when I accidentally flashed the mark when I hugged Sarah. I know, because I checked straight after to make sure no one saw anything."

"Okay, he saw the mark on your wrist and wants to help you with the demons." I pulled my seatbelt across my chest, clicked it in place, and started the truck. "We can work with that. I mean, if he—"

"Wait, it gets weirder." Talia tugged at her seatbelt's shoulder strap and adjusted her position in the passenger seat, putting her back to the door. "He said he knows how to remove it."

"What?" I jammed on the brakes and threw the gear shift into park. This conversation required my full attention. "How in the hell would he know how to do that?"

"That's what I was hoping to find out, but then he started giving off a creeper vibe and my wolf was having none of it." The corner of her mouth curved upward in a lopsided grin. "Your timing was impeccable."

"I try." I met her smile with one of my own and unfastened my seatbelt, turning in my seat to mirror her position. "Did he give you any clues about the mark or how to remove it?"

"No, and I didn't get the impression that he would just hand over the information. It was like he wanted to be the hero or something." She twisted her long golden hair into a loose bun at the base of her neck and tucked a stray strand behind her ears. "I told him about the coven, that they were going to help us. He doesn't think they can. The whole thing was just so odd."

"Speaking of the coven, Marguerite has agreed to help, but she needs to examine the mark first." I tugged at the sleeve of the sweatshirt I'd let her borrow, struggling to ignore the way our scents mingled together, and inched up the sleeve to expose the demon mark.

It wasn't healing, which for a wolf shifter with accelerated healing ability, was odd. The blisters that made up the demonic symbol were still raised and red.

"The sooner you see Marguerite, the better." I put the truck in gear and headed for the coven's encampment on the other side of the property. "Removing the mark is top priority and the coven seems like our best bet. We'll keep an eye on Darius, but I don't think he really knows how to remove the mark."

"That's a bold statement to make if he couldn't follow through. Why would he even say that?"

Bewilderment clouded Talia's beautiful eyes.

"I can think of a reason." I couldn't help myself. I lifted a hand and ran my thumb over her cheek, down and around her jawline.

She shivered beneath my touch, but the warmth in her eyes showed me she wasn't repulsed. Her mouth parted slightly, and her teeth gently nibbled on her bottom lip, igniting instant heat in my groin.

I shifted in my seat. Now was not the time for desire to rear up, but when it came to Talia, everything about her made my senses switch into overdrive.

She dropped her gaze, breathing slightly faster than she had moments earlier, and I chuckled wryly. "We should get back," I said, reluctance obvious in my voice.

She nodded without looking up. "Uh huh. Yes. Good idea."

I turned my attention to the road. Talia didn't see the qualities I did when I looked at her. Qualities that went beyond physical beauty, though she was stunning. It was her quiet strength, the kindness in her eyes and heart, that drew me to her.

After what she'd been through with her ex and her old pack, it was no wonder she undervalued her worth.

She needed a reminder of how beautiful she was, inside and out. I wanted to be the man to do that for her, make her see how perfect she was, but my heart had been closed off for so long, I wasn't sure if I could open up again. Not to the extent she deserved.

But she made me want to try.

"I want to help the pack." Talia pulled me from my thoughts, saving me from dwelling too long on the past and on things I couldn't change. "I'd like to be put on rotation for a watch. It doesn't matter which one or who you pair me with. Put me where you need me."

"You don't have to. The pack—"

"No. After everything the pack has done for me, it's the least I can do." She reached over and rested her hand on my forearm, giving a gentle squeeze. "I want to do this. I need to do this. So, please, Galen, put me where you need me most."

What if where I need you most is by my side?

"Okay, I'll talk to David and see what we can come up with. I'm sure there's a few spots that still need to be filled."

"Thank you so much." She beamed at me. Happiness radiated from the passenger seat, filling the cab, and permeating my senses.

It was infectious. *She* was infectious.

I parked the truck outside Marguerite's tent, but I didn't open my door. Instead, I reached over the console, cupped the left side of Talia's face in my hand, and leaned over to her. It seemed that I just couldn't stop touching her. She rubbed her face against my palm and this time, closed the remaining distance between us.

Her lips found mine, parting when I groaned and deepened the kiss. She crawled over the console onto my lap and straddled my hips. My cock hardened and it was all I could do to control myself as she pressed against my flesh.

I trailed my hands over her ribs and around to her back, sliding lower until I cupped her gorgeous rounded ass and urged her even closer.

The tiny mewling sound that escaped her drove me wild, spurring me on.

Then her hands were somehow beneath my shirt, warm fingers curling against my naked chest. I groaned as all my blood headed south. She drove me fucking crazy—in the best possible way.

Someone rapped on the window, the face and figure distorted through the condensation we'd managed to build up on the glass.

When I focused properly, it was Sarah. "Uh, sorry to interrupt." The witch feigned a cough to hide her amusement. "Marguerite is needed at the main gate to help with the reinforcement of the wards. So, if you want her to look at Talia's mark, you better come inside now."

"I guess we better go in." Talia rested her head on my shoulder and nuzzled into the crook of my neck. The warmth of her breath against the sensitive spot raised goosebumps on my skin.

"Yeah. I guess so."

Talia climbed back to the passenger side and got out of the truck.

"You coming?" She laughed, catching the double entendre after the words left her mouth. "Don't answer—"

"I was hoping to." I flashed her a mischievous smile and winked before flicking my gaze down to my lap and adjusting myself. These jeans were damn tight. "You go ahead. I need a minute."

She raked her gaze downward and pulled her bottom lip between her teeth.

"Not helping, Talia."

"Sorry." Her laughter as she shut the passenger door said she was anything but.

The sway of her hips as she followed Sarah inside Marguerite's tent didn't help my situation either.

The witches needed to come up with a way to remove Talia's mark, and fast. If something happened to her, I'd never forgive myself.

Talia deserved a happily ever after, and I was going to do everything in my power to see that she got it.

SIX

TALIA

Marguerite examined the mark and sketched a copy of the symbol in a leather-bound journal. She questioned me about the attack and took particular interest in the physical characteristics of the demon.

I wished I'd paid better attention. My description lacked detail and left her with more questions than answers.

At the time, I'd been more concerned with staying alive than the color of the demon's eyes or scars marking his body.

She believed the solution to my problem, removing the demon mark and any claim he may have had on me, lay in uncovering his identity. According to Marguerite, we needed to summon the demon and force him to remove the mark while he was bound inside a summoning circle.

But to do that we needed his name.

Easier said than done. It wasn't like there was a demon directory where we could just look him up. She assured me that once she finished with the wards, translating the symbol and locating the demon would become her top priorities.

It was hard to say who was more disappointed, me or Galen. He stormed out of Marguerite's tent and waited in his truck while I said my goodbyes, and apologized for his misdirected anger.

"No need to apologize, dear. I didn't take it personally." Marguerite took me by the hand and ushered me out of her tent. "Galen is a friend and ally. His feelings for you run deep and that scares him. So does the prospect of losing you before he has the chance to make you his."

Make me his?

The idea sent an immediate frisson of desire down my spine.

When I returned to the truck, I sat in the passenger seat with my hands folded in my lap and stared out the side window as we drove back toward Galen's house. I watched the coven's encampment get smaller while I considered what Marguerite had said about Galen's feelings for me.

He was physically attracted to me. That much was clear, but the rest of his feelings were muddied and left me confused. Whenever we got close to intimacy on an emotional level, I felt him pull away.

Something was holding him back.

Marguerite said he was scared, and I assumed that had something to do with his ex. I'd yet to hear the whole story, but I knew all too well about bad breakups and had my own scars to prove it.

Clearly, we both needed to work on resolving our past if we wanted to have a future.

Galen drove me home, escorted me inside, and checked the house for any sign of demons. After a thorough search of every room, he seemed satisfied I was safe—at least for now—and went for a quick visit with his father before heading out for his turn on watch.

That became our routine for seven uneventful days.

He split his time between his duties protecting the pack lands and checking in on me and Max. The bond he had with his father was a painful reminder that my father had been taken from me too soon. I missed my dad, and the need for vengeance grew stronger with each passing day.

The demons continued their attack on the town but kept their distance from the pack lands—and our house. The witches had obviously done a great job with their warding.

Last night, before he'd headed out on his watch, Galen expressed concern for the coven. One of the witches who refused to relocate, choosing to stand her ground with the townspeople instead, had been afflicted by the effects of a demon, driving her insane. He worried about the witches under his protection, and whether he could keep them safe from the demons' effects.

I killed time waiting for my first watch by taking care of Max and tackling a few overdue chores. The alpha said his house had never been so clean, but I could only rearrange the furniture so many times.

When the day for my shift on watch arrived, I was bouncing off the walls and driving Max crazy. The poor man needed his rest and that was hard to come by while I was dragging a love seat from one side of the living room to the other.

"Talia!" He called out from his bedroom.

I cringed at the slight annoyance in his tone and went straight to his room. "Yes, alpha?"

"You need to calm down a little. I know you're going stir crazy in here, but don't you have a watch shift tonight?"

I nodded. "Yeah... I do."

"Great," he said with a grin. "How about you go for a walk? Or... something?"

He was as ready for me to get out of the house as I was.

I chuckled. "Yes Max."

I was tying my sneakers when Galen walked in through the back door and set his keys on the kitchen counter. "Hey, there. I thought you would have headed out already."

"I'm leaving in a few minutes. Erica offered to walk with me." I tossed my phone and keys into my bag and hitched it over my shoulder. "Your dad's awake. I just checked in on him and let him know I was leaving."

A knock on the front door had me smiling.

"That must be Erica." I made my way through the kitchen and living room, heading for the front door.

Galen cut me off midstride.

"Let me check." He strode to the window, pulled back the curtain, and peered outside. His posture softened and he offered a quick wave before closing the curtain. "It's Erica."

He was more protective than usual. Marguerite hadn't made any progress on deciphering the symbol which meant we still hadn't learned the demon's name. Galen was worried something would happen to me before she figured it out.

I was worried he had too much on his plate and was spreading himself too thin.

It was a vicious cycle.

"I'll see you tomorrow." He looked so worried, I stepped up to him and cupped my hands around his face, before pulling him in for a quick kiss. "Make sure your dad finishes his protein shake, please."

"It tastes like chalk," Max called out from his bedroom.

"You're going to drink it anyway and quit eavesdropping," I called back.

Galen chuckled and shook his head. He trailed his hand down my arm, taking my hand in his, and tugged me back for one more kiss. "Be careful, okay?"

Erica knocked again. "You coming?"

"I'm always careful." I smiled and bounded for the door. "I'll be fine. Stop worrying."

"I don't think I can. Not where you're concerned."

He was making it almost impossible to leave, but I managed to blow him a kiss and close the door behind me.

"Come on, let's go. We're going to be late, and Markus is going to be pissed."

"Sorry," I said as I jumped off the patio and walked alongside her at a hurried pace. "Galen came by to check in on his dad and we got to talking."

"You mean, Galen came by to check up on you." Erica jabbed me with her elbow and laughed as we marched toward the meeting hall.

"That too." I sighed.

"Hey, I was just kidding around. It's pretty obvious Galen's got it bad for you, but no one holds that against you. Well, there's probably some single ladies in the pack who might." Erica snorted when she saw my scowl, and tried in vain to rein in her laughter.

"Great," I grumbled. I didn't like the sound of any other woman being interested in Galen. It raised my wolf's hackles and made her distinctly uneasy.

Markus was waiting for us when we reached the town hall. He glanced at his watch. "You're late."

"Blame Galen." Erica winked and jerked her head in my direction.

I groaned and glanced away into the forest. The two of them shared another laugh at my expense.

The ribbing didn't bother me. I'd experienced worse from my old alpha, the man who would have been my father-in-law if I'd married Maddox. Besides, I knew that it was all in good fun. Erica and Markus were just joking around.

"I need you on the south side." He indicated a box next to the front door of the town hall where we could leave our clothes if and when we shifted. "Go on, get out of here."

"So, how do you want to do this?" I spoke with Erica, not rushing to undress since we hadn't yet decided our plan of action.

"If we split up, we'll cover more ground. I'll head west, and you can run the line east." Erica bent her knee and raised her leg back, hooking her hand on her foot, and stretched out her hamstrings.

We both opted for two legs and not four, making communication easier if we came across something suspicious. I slid my cell in the phone slot of my leggings and tucked my purse into the clothes box with my sweater.

"Check-in in fifteen?" Erica set a timer on her phone, stowed it away inside her sports bra, and took off in a westerly direction.

I pulled my phone back out and set the timer before I headed east.

The pack's property was beautiful, having just the right amount of pasture and wooded areas to create the perfect habitat for wolves—and small prey.

No wonder my old alpha had been so desperate to steal the land from Galen and his father. He'd been a terrible steward to the lands owned by his pack during his tenure as alpha and needed better hunting grounds.

What my former pack needs is a better alpha.

Leaves crunched on the forest floor just outside the property line to my left, followed by the snap of a branch.

I smelled her before I saw her. Natasha. She was my best friend Celia's older sister. We'd kinda grown up together, but Natasha didn't love me the way Celia did.

Natasha's wolf breached the boundary. She bared her fangs, snarling as she squatted back on her haunches. Then she launched, going straight for my throat.

She'd wasted the element of surprise with all the noise she'd made tromping the woods. I was ready for her attack.

I clocked her with a roundhouse kick to her ribs, knocking her out of the air and onto the ground with a meaty thump. She pushed herself onto all fours, but she favored her right front paw when she circled around me, testing for weakness in my defenses.

She should have been thinking about her own.

I kicked her injured paw hard enough to elicit a yelp and punched her upside the ear. She dropped to her belly, lowered her head, and whimpered her submission.

"What are you doing here, Natasha?" I rested my hands on my hips. "We clearly can't have a conversation like this, so go ahead and shift back."

Natasha shifted from the sleek white wolf to a five-foot-seven platinum blond. I envied her curves. I did not, however, envy her predicament.

"Well?" I tapped my foot, but the grass tamped the sound and dulled the effect. "How many more are there?"

"It's just me." She raised her hands in a placating gesture. "I swear it. He sent me here to scout the boundary and if I saw you, I was supposed to take you out."

"Well, Maddox and the alpha are going to be really disappointed because you're a terrible scout and a worse assassin." I pulled out my phone and texted Erica.

"I think we both know that I wasn't really trying, Talia." Natasha scoffed and crossed her arms over her midsection.

As much as it pained me to admit it, she was right. I'd seen Natasha in action, and she was a gifted hunter and fighter. She held her own against the larger wolves in my old pack and earned her place as scout and once upon a time, my friend.

But that felt like a lifetime ago.

"Fine. You were holding back." I spared a glance over my shoulder in search of Erica.

The pent-up tension eased from my neck and shoulders when her gray coat broke through the shadows of the trees. She must have shifted to get to me faster.

"So, why even show yourself if you weren't going to follow through with the attack?" I slid my phone back in my pocket to keep my hands free in case she decided to get squirrely on me.

"You caught my scent." She shrugged as if that explained everything.

In a way, I supposed it did.

Erica burst onto the scene, tongue out one side of her mouth and panting. She padded up beside me and sat back on her haunches next to my leg. Her presence added to my strength and made it easier to confront Natasha—and my past.

"So, why did you pull your punches? What could you possibly have to gain by failing your mission?" I couldn't wrap my head around why she would choose to do such a thing.

"Not everyone in the pack wants you dead, Talia." She raised her head, jutted her chin, and met my glacial gaze.

"Why, because they miss me? Like they wanted me to be a member of the pack? Yeah okay, Natasha. Go peddle that bullshit somewhere else. I'm not buying it." I refused to believe anyone in my old pack could have a change of heart.

Even Natasha, who I thought was my friend, didn't stick up for me in the end. She'd stood by and watched as the alpha threw me away. She didn't even say goodbye when I left.

"I didn't say they wanted you back. Just that they don't want you dead." Natasha jerked her thumb toward the tree line. "Can I get my clothes? It's a little chilly out here."

Erica took off in the direction Natasha pointed, tracked her scent to where she'd stashed her clothes, and trotted back with a bundle in her mouth.

"The alpha and maybe half a dozen loyalists are the only ones pushing for your death. The rest of the pack was satisfied with your banishment. But there were a few who opposed that as well, like my sister. And Nyssa, of course." Natasha stepped into her jeans, hiked the denim over her long legs, and buttoned them at the waist.

That sounded more like the pack I knew. They had no use for me and didn't want me around. At least the majority of them didn't want me dead. The fact that Natasha disobeyed an order meant my old alpha was losing his hold over the pack.

"I should have stood up or spoken up or... I don't know, done something." Natasha slid her arms through the sleeves of a navy-blue cotton shirt and tugged it over her head. "I'm really sorry, Talia."

"You didn't even come see me before I left. Not standing up to the alpha I understood, but the cold shoulder? You totally blew me off like we were never friends, Natasha." I tried to hide my pain, but the wound was still too fresh, too raw, for me to cover it up.

"The alpha threatened banishment for anyone who tried to help you or show you any kindness."

I glared at her. "That didn't stop Celia or Nyssa from helping me."

Natasha shoved her hands in the front pockets of her jeans and rocked back on her heels. "I don't have anything outside of the pack."

"Neither did I."

If I sounded bitter, it was because I was.

"I know it doesn't make it better, any of it, but I am sorry for what happened to you and that I didn't step up in any way to support you."

Natasha's apology was my first step toward closure.

"I'm sorry, too." I raised my hand in response to the confused look on her face and to stave off any questions she wanted to ask. "Because this attack can't go unanswered. I have to call it in with Galen's beta."

Erica huffed her approval.

I pulled out my phone and dialed Markus's number.

"We have a situation on the southern boundary," I said when he answered.

Natasha's fate was out of my hands. She'd crossed pack lines and invaded Galen's territory. She would have to answer for that.

And so would her alpha. He wanted me dead and refused to stop trying. I wanted justice for my father's murder. Only one of us would get what we wanted.

I just hoped it was going to be me.

CHAPTER

SEVEN

GALEN

"What's on your mind, son?" My father dug his elbows into the mattress and inched himself up into a sitting position. He was as pale as the sheets around him and the dark smudges beneath his eyes spoke of a desperate need for sleep.

"Why does there have to be something on my mind? I wanted to spend some time with you." I handed him the remote from the nightstand beside the bed.

"I'm your father. You think I can't tell when something is bothering you? I can read you like a book." His raspy laugh turned into a cough.

"Okay, okay, don't get yourself riled up." I picked up the pitcher and refilled his glass of water. "I'll talk."

His eyes softened and the corners of his mouth upturned in a gentle smile. He sucked down half the glass of water through the bendy straw as I held it in front of him.

"It's about Talia." I set the glass back on the table and plopped down into the wooden chair beside his bed.

"Of course, it is." He leaned back on the pillows and closed his eyes. "You've never needed my advice for pack business."

"I ask for it anyway. Just because I don't need it, doesn't mean I don't want to hear it."

"Good, because I have plenty left to give. Now, tell me about Talia. What's bothering you?" His eyes were still closed, but I knew I had his full attention.

"Where do I even start?" I raked my fingers through my hair, tugging at the roots. "She's driving me crazy, and I mean that in a good way. I just never expected to—"

"Have feelings for her? Especially after you kidnapped her with the half-cocked plan to sell her back to her old pack." He wrapped his arms around his midsection and stifled a laugh. "What's really unexpected is that she has feelings for you."

"Wow. Thanks, Dad." I knew he was just kidding around, but his words stung a little—probably because they held a ring of truth.

"The biggest thing standing in your way of happiness is you, Galen." He clutched one of the extra pillows to his chest, rolled to his side, and coughed until he was gasping for air.

I hated seeing my father that way. He shouldn't have gotten sick. Wolf shifters didn't get sick and yet there he was, lying in a makeshift hospital bed in his bedroom. It didn't make any sense.

Nothing made sense. Not his illness, the pack territory war, the demons or Talia's mark. "I'll take your silence as confirmation that I'm right." He turned back over to face me, his eyes wet with tears from his coughing fit, and reached for my hand. "You need to let go of the past, Galen. You would risk life and limb for our pack. You're going to have to risk your heart for love. Trust me, it'll be worth it, if you can bring yourself to let down that wall you've built around your emotions."

"Thanks, Dad." I squeezed his hand and held on a little longer than usual. I wasn't ready to let him go. "You always know what to say."

His grip had weakened along with his pulse. The illness had been killing him slowly, eating away at his strength, and it seemed that its appetite had grown. Whatever virus had him in its grip had doubled its efforts to devour him, body and soul.

I made sure he was comfortable, had plenty more water and his cell phone within arm's reach before I headed back outside.

My phone blew up with text messages before I made it out to my truck. They were all from David. Which meant we had trouble.

"We've got a problem," he said, in lieu of a greeting when I called him.

"What kind of a problem?" I began jogging up the main road toward the center of town.

"A five-foot-seven, one-hundred-and twenty-pound, bleached blond kind of problem."

David's response caught me off guard. I'd expected him to mention another demon attack or a cursed witch who'd gone insane.

"Trouble on the first date?" I joked, turning left at the fork and heading up the hill.

I didn't normally make light of any situation where David called me, but with one emergency after another, I had to find the humor where I could.

"You're hilarious, and no. It was trouble on someone's first watch." David called out orders to run the perimeter again to a wolf in the background.

Talia. My heart lurched. "Son of a bitch. I knew it was a bad idea to put her on watch. I might as well have strung a slab of meat from her neck and rung the dinner bell." I began to run. "Is she hurt?"

"Talia's fine. The blond, on the other hand, is a bit worse for wear, with a few cuts and bruises. Nothing that won't heal with a shift. Listen, before you go off the handle, try to remember that Talia's a grown woman and just wants to help the pack."

David was more than my second in command; he was my confidant and friend.

I trusted his advice almost as much as my father's.

"Yeah, I know, but I don't want her to get hurt. If something happens to her…" I didn't even want to think about it and tried to push the thought from my mind.

"Now who's the one having dating problems?" David said with a chuckle. "I'll meet you out the front."

The blond must have been from Talia's old pack. Pretty brazen to actually come onto our lands to attack her.

It was an act of war, and I would respond accordingly.

As promised, David was at the front door of the meeting hall to greet me as I ran up to the porch.

"Where's Talia?"

"Still at the southern boundary with Markus and Erica, keeping an eye on the prisoner."

"Son of a bitch sends an assassin into our land to kill someone under our protection." I flicked my gaze to David then back to the gravel-covered road. "This attack can't go unanswered."

"I don't think he expected this so-called assassin to succeed. According to Talia, she didn't put up much of a fight." David scratched the stubble along his jaw. "Honestly, I think he expected her to get captured or killed."

"He's challenging me." My wolf stalked to the surface, his growl rattling my ribcage. He was ready for a fight. That made two of us. "I'm sure he'll be pleased to hear that I accept."

"You need to up the stakes. Put an end to this shit once and for all. We've got enough trouble with the demons."

"I know. We're spreading ourselves too thin, protecting the witches, fighting off a rival pack, and dealing with demons." I tilted my head to indicate I wanted to get walking, and David stepped into place beside me. "We can't keep this up forever."

"You already know the solution to one of our problems." David gave voice to my thoughts.

"A challenge to the death."

Like my father had said, life or limb.

I was ready to do whatever it took to keep my pack safe. Except tell Talia my plan. She had enough to worry about with the demon mark. She needed to focus on working with the witches to get it removed.

David's torch illuminated three people and one wolf near the pack's side of the property markers: Talia, Markus, a woman I assumed was the assassin, and Erica still in her wolf form.

I jogged over to them and Talia rushed into my open arms. I wrapped myself around her, holding her close, and breathed her in.

This situation could have turned out differently. I could have lost her.

"I'm fine, Galen. There's not a scratch on me." Talia returned my embrace and squeezed her arms around my midsection. It was tough to actually let her go, but in the end I had to.

"Want to introduce me to your *friend?*" I brushed a light kiss across her forehead and untangled myself from her arms.

"It's funny you say that. Once upon a time, Natasha was my friend." Talia's voice held a bitter edge.

I hated that she'd gone through something that made her feel that her friends had turned on her. I couldn't change her past, but maybe, just maybe, I could protect her from that in the future.

"What are we going to do with her, Galen?" Markus held Natasha's hands behind her back while Erica sat at attention by his feet.

"Well, after sending her on this little suicide mission, I'd say it's pretty clear her alpha doesn't want her back." As I started walking over to the rival wolf, Talia slipped her tiny hand in mine. I gripped her tight, enjoying the connection. "Do you have anything to say for yourself?"

"I took the assignment but never planned on going through with it. I needed to get a message to Talia. She needed to know that the whole pack isn't out for her blood." Natasha lowered her head and averted her gaze in a show of submission.

"So, you're just a messenger?" I stepped forward, closing the distance between us, and exerted my dominance as alpha. "I'm supposed to believe that bullshit?"

"Believe what you want. Dying by your hand is better than living under his thumb." Natasha bucked the natural instinct to submit to an alpha, raised her head, and met my gaze.

The defiance only lasted a moment before she dropped her head again, but the steely determination I saw in her eyes gave me pause. If she had disobeyed the orders of her alpha to reach out to Talia, then killing her would be an unnecessary and unjustified death.

"Take her the meeting house," I said to Markus. "Erica can babysit her until I decide what to do with her." I wanted to speak to Talia in private, hear her side of the story and gauge what she thought about Natasha's intentions. "David, get a hold of Theo. Take Markus with you once everything is squared up at the meeting house and fill them in on what we discussed in the truck. I need to talk to Talia."

I waited for everyone to leave before following behind with Talia. She seemed distant, all of a sudden, as if she expected to be reprimanded for what had happened on her watch.

"I'm not upset with you, Talia." I draped my arm around her shoulder, tucking her against my side, and felt the tension in her body relax slightly. "Quite the opposite. I'm worried sick something will happen to you, and I won't be able to stop it."

"I know that's why you don't want me to take my turn at watch, but I can handle it, Galen." She held the hand I had draped over her shoulder and cuddled closer. "I can't just sit around and pace the floors waiting to hear something from Marguerite. I *need* to do something."

"I know you do." I kissed her forehead and focused on walking in the dark. "You have David to thank for being added to the watch, by the way. He talked some sense into me. Given the fact that your old alpha is actively sending people to kill you, would it be too much to ask that you stick with your partner and not split up?"

"I can do that." Talia beamed a thousand-watt smile at the news that she would still be on the watch rotation. "So, what's going to happen to Natasha?"

"That's what I wanted to talk to you about."

"Me?" Her smile faded and her eyes widened. "You want *my* opinion on how to handle the situation?"

"Of course, I do." I steered her around a tree and kept our walk at a strolling pace so no one could overhear us. "You have a history with Natasha. One that's different from the history I have with her pack."

"Well, the rose-colored glasses are off. The day I left I saw the blood and rust on the relationships that had previously mattered to me." Her cheeks flushed and her pulse quickened with an obviously rising temper. "But for what its worth, I don't think Natasha was lying."

"I don't either. I can usually sniff out a lie, and her words rang true to me." I shook my head and let out a frustrated sigh. "And therein lies the problem."

"I don't think she deserves a death sentence, Galen." Talia slid her hand from mine and rubbed her palms against her thighs. "There are plenty of people in that pack who deserve to die, but Natasha isn't one of them."

"Well, that's what will happen to her if I send her back." I closed my eyes and pinched the bridge of my nose. "I guess I better find a more suitable place to hold a prisoner than the meeting house."

"Galen." Talia twisted the hem of her shirt around her fingers. "I want to be the one to kill him."

It looked like I would be having a conversation with Talia about the challenge sooner than I'd planned. Which, prior to this moment, had been never.

"Listen, I know better than most how much you want justice—"

"He used my father as a scapegoat for his mistakes and then killed him in cold blood. I don't want justice. I want *revenge*." Her tone was fierce. She sucked in a breath between her teeth and grabbed her marked wrist, then winced. "Ouch."

"What is it? What's wrong?" I reached for her arm, but she jerked back.

"Don't touch it. It burns." She cradled her arm to her chest and rocked where she stood, groaning. "Why is it burning? Oh God, make it stop."

Her arm went limp suddenly, and she stopped rocking. Her eyelids fluttered shut and her head lolled forward, pulling her body with it. I jumped for her, and even with my shifter speed I only just managed to catch her before she hit the dirt.

What the fuck?

"Talia?" I turned her over and and cradled her in my arms. "Talia, can you hear me?"

I braced her head in the crook of my arm and checked her pulse. It was strong and steady. I watched the rise and fall of her chest for any signs of difficulty breathing but she seemed fine—apart from being suddenly unconscious.

I had no idea what had happened to her.

"Talia, wake up, baby."

My sleeping beauty didn't stir. Was this related to the demon mark? Would she ever wake up again?

CHAPTER

EIGHT

GALEN

I t had been several minutes and Talia was still unconscious no matter how hard I tried to wake her. I held her against my body and reached for my cell phone.

I dialed David's number, hoping that he and Markus had already connected with Theo. It was easier to update them all at once. David answered on the first ring, put me on speaker, and I briefed my betas on the situation.

"The witches better have a solution," I said. "It's been well over a week since Marguerite has given any updates and Talia is running out of time."

"Keep us posted, Galen," David said.

I ended the call and hauled ass across the property to the coven's encampment.

I ran in the direction of Marguerite's tent, skidding on the gravel and almost falling with my precious baggage.

Marguerite peeked out the flap to her tent and her eyes widened when she saw me carrying Talia. "Galen, while I always enjoy your visits, this clearly isn't a social call." She held the tent flap open. "Why don't you come inside?"

"Something is wrong with her." I rushed forward, hoisting Talia's limp body over my shoulder in a fireman's carry before bringing her inside Marguerite's tent.

"Oh, my goddess, you should have called me immediately. What happened?" Marguerite rushed around her tent, gathering herbs and dried flowers.

"We were just walking in the forest, talking. Someone from her old pack attacked tonight and she was upset." I adjusted my hold on Talia and cradled her in my arms.

Her breathing was normal, but she still showed no signs of waking.

"The mark on her arm started burning. She was in a lot of pain, Marguerite, and then she just passed out." I brushed a few strands of Talia's golden hair from her face and pressed a kiss to her temple.

Marguerite walked over to a bookshelf and blew on the wicks of three large white candles that sat on one of the shelves. The flames flickered to life. She piled chunks of charred wood beneath a small cauldron on a massive wood-planked kitchen table and lit the fire with a snap of her fingers.

"How long has she been this way?" She rifled through various jars next to the cauldron, knocking some of them over in her haste to find whatever stray ingredient she was looking for.

"Not long. Maybe ten minutes. We were at the opposite end of the property. I came straight here as fast as I could."

Shit. This was like Jessie all over again. Hurt and in trouble, and I couldn't do a thing to save her. Was I cursed to lose the women I loved in a violent or traumatic way? Was it some cruel twist of fate? Or karma?

"Set her down over there." Marguerite pointed to a cot in the corner. She grabbed a wooden spoon from a jar stuffed with utensils in the middle of the table.

I did as I was told without argument or question—something I wasn't used to doing as my father's son, the next alpha of our pack.

But I would have done anything she said, even bartered my soul, if it meant saving Talia.

"Tilt her head back and open her mouth." Marguerite ladled her concoction into a small silver pitcher, grabbed the folds of her dress to raise the hem off the floor, and hurried to Talia's side.

She poured the thick liquid from the pitcher straight down Talia's throat.

"What if she chokes?" I asked.

It had been years since I'd felt this helpless. Not since Jessie, and the weight of the guilt I carried in my heart ever since she'd died, seemed quadrupled when it came to Talia. The emotions came rushing back, amplified, and threatening to pull me down through the ground to the depths of despair.

I wondered if Marguerite had a potion that could make me forget certain parts of my past—or at least one part in particular.

"Have a little faith, Galen. I'm high priestess for a reason."

Marguerite slowed the flow of the potion, letting gravity and nature take their course, then emptied the remaining contents of the pitcher into Talia's mouth. She pressed her palm against Talia's forehead and chanted something in a language that sounded like Latin.

Why are these spells always Latin? Spanish I can follow.

Talia shot upright on the cot, her eyes wide. She sucked in a deep, gasping breath.

I rushed forward to grab her but Marguerite thrust out her arm, blocking me from picking Talia up and crushing her to my chest. "Let the girl breathe."

"Right, sorry." I gave Talia the space she needed to come to her senses fully.

Seconds later her eyes focused properly on me and she smiled. "Galen." She took my hand, tugging me close. I sat beside her on the cot as she scrunched up her face and took in her surroundings. "Marguerite?"

"What do you remember, dear?" The high priestess pulled a

ladder-backed wooden chair out from a small dining table and dragged it over so she could sit by the side of the cot.

"Galen and I were talking." Talia turned round, sapphire eyes on me. A frown marred her brow. "And then... how did we end up here?"

"It's okay. I'll explain everything in a minute. Just tell Marguerite what you do remember, all right? Then I'll fill in the gaps." I squeezed her hand to reassure her that I wasn't going anywhere and she had my support.

"I don't remember anything after that." Talia shook her head, her strawberry-blond locks swishing on her shoulders. "There was just burning. Intense burning, like my skin was on fire, and then it was all black."

"You were upset, talking about your father and wanting vengeance. You said you wanted to kill your old alpha." I directed my question at Marguerite. "Is it... reacting to her emotions?"

"Let's hope not." She pressed her lips into a pencil-thin line, and her brows pinched together.

"Why, what does that mean?" Talia swung her legs over the side of the cot and got to her feet despite my protests. "What aren't you telling me, Marguerite?"

"You're familiar with a rancher's brand on a herd of cattle?" Marguerite's question was rhetorical, so she plunged ahead without a pause. "A demon's brand is nothing like that. The rancher marks the cattle and that's the end of it. But a demon... when one of them marks you..."

"I'm connected to it?" Talia turned her arm and stared down at the mark on her wrist. "Right then. Cut it out, like a cancer. Once you get it all, I'll shift and heal."

"If I thought that would work, I would have operated when Galen first brought you to me." Marguerite rested her hands on Talia's shoulders, as if to calm her growing agitation. "The mark is part of the demon and now part of you. It's an open connection between the two of you, and it grows stronger with every passing day."

"So, remove the fucking thing," I snapped, my temper getting the better of me. "You were supposed to have figured out a way to do that already."

I was furious that this was the first we'd heard about the open connection between Talia and the demon.

"Galen, I understand that you're—"

"No, Marguerite, I don't think you do understand." I felt my hold on my wolf slip. He was close to the surface and ready to break free.

"We still don't know the name of the demon that Talia is connected to. We need that name. There is one thing I can try but I can't make any promises that it will remove the mark." Marguerite retrieved an old leather tome from a bookshelf on the far side of the room.

"I really don't understand witches. If there's something you can try, then why haven't you tried it already?" I growled, my hands curled into fists at my side.

"You're under a great deal of stress, wolf. So, I'll give you a pass this time, but let me remind you that I am the alpha equivalent among witches and deserve the same level of respect and decorum as your wolves grant you. Do you understand?"

The air crackled with electricity and the lights inside her tent flickered. I recognized the flash of power in her eyes. It was similar to the change in my eyes when I shifted.

Marguerite was not a witch to trifle with and I had overstepped my bounds with someone I considered a friend and ally.

Talia's gaze ping-ponged between us, worry fluttering across her face.

"You're right. Please accept my apologies." I dipped my head and bent at the waist into a slight bow. "This isn't your fault, and I shouldn't be directing my frustrations at you."

Talia released a small sigh of relief and gave me an appreciative smile.

"The reason I'm not throwing spells or potions at the mark with the hopes that one of them will work, is because I don't want to make Talia's situation worse—which is a very real possibility." Marguerite flipped through the pages of her grimoire.

"But you're willing to try it now?" Talia's voice cracked as she spoke. Her bottom lip quivered and her eyes watered.

I wanted to scoop her up and surround her with my essence, until no one could hurt her anymore.

"I am, yes." Marguerite set the open tome on a bookstand and went about collecting more ingredients from her stores. "But you need to be willing to accept the risk."

"The risk?" My query was sharp, despite my previous apology.

Marguerite stared at me calmly. "The risk that we make it worse."

I opened my mouth to speak, then realized it was up to Talia to make the call. It was her body, and it had to be her choice. But she didn't need to do this alone. "I'm here with you, Talia." I pulled her into a side hug. "Whatever you decide."

Talia closed her eyes and relaxed into me. "Thank you, Galen. That means more than you realize." She took a deep breath, opened her eyes and looked at Marguerite. "Okay. Let's do it."

We waited for what felt like an eternity for Marguerite to finish preparing and cooking her spell.

Talia cringed as Marguerite slathered the gelatinous substance over Talia's wrist. The witch hovered her hand over the demon's mark and made counterclockwise circles while she spoke and then repeated an incantation. Over and over.

Nothing bad happened. Nothing good happened, either.

Marguerite released her hold on Talia's arm and took a step back. "I'm sorry. I hoped this would work."

"You tried," I said, and I meant it. "We're all in unchartered territory. We'll figure this out."

I hope.

This was another failed experiment and another setback. At the rate things were going, Talia would be claimed by the demon, and I would lose her forever.

Or maybe not.

"What about Darius?" I turned to face Talia and rested my hands on her shoulders. "He told you he knew how to remove the demon's mark, didn't he?"

"Yes, but—"

"Then we should call him. See what he has to say." I pulled my phone out of my jeans pocket and scrolled through my contacts list in search of Darius.

"Galen, I don't want to call Darius." Talia grabbed my hand and pulled it away from my phone, stopping me from swiping the touch screen.

"Who is this Darius person?" Marguerite returned the grimoire to its place on her bookshelf and set about cleaning her cauldron and spelling equipment.

"A new member of my pack who appears to have a thing for Talia. It's probably bullshit, but he claims to know how to get rid of the mark. If he does have information, we need to find out what it is."

I expected Marguerite to agree that it was a lead worth pursuing.

"I think we need to ask ourselves where Darius would have gained this information." Marguerite poured herself a glass of wine and sat down in her wooden chair.

"Who cares where he heard it from?" I didn't understand the reluctance. "As long as we can get the mark off Talia's wrist, that's what matters, right?"

"That's a double-edged question, Galen." Marguerite took a long draw of wine from her cup and set it down on a small table that floated over to her from the front corner of her tent. "Knowledge is power. Especially this kind of knowledge."

"It's not like he could just stroll into the local library and find it in the reference section." Talia looked to Marguerite for confirmation. "Right? He couldn't do that, could he?"

"No, it's most certainly not in any library this side of hell." Marguerite polished off the wine in her glass and dabbed the corners of her mouth with a cloth napkin. I noted that she hadn't offered any to Talia or me. Not that we'd likely feel like drinking it right now, but still, would have been nice to offer! "So again, where would he get the information?"

"You think he's just posturing, trying to get closer to Talia? Make himself seem important?" I scowled and shoved my phone back in my pocket.

"It doesn't matter why," Talia said. "I don't trust him, Galen. I get a bad feeling whenever I'm around him. Like, stalker vibes." She shivered.

Stalker vibes? What the hell? Had I let the wrong shifter in to my own pack?

"Okay, I admit defeat." I raised my hands in surrender. "It's pretty obvious I'm outnumbered on this one."

I had to trust them. Talia had great instincts and they'd kept her alive so far. I made a mental note to keep a much closer eye on Darius from this point forward.

"Thank you for not forcing the issue." Talia reached for me, grabbed me by the shirt and tugged me closer. Then she pressed a kiss against my lips.

It was sweet, and simple, and perfect.

We lingered over the kiss, which felt so gentle, and yet, incited so much emotion in my chest. Eventually we pulled apart, and her gaze connected with mine, promising so much. If we could only get past our current crises.

"So, now what?" I felt like we were back to square one.

"I think we need to convene with an expert in demon matters." Marguerite looked like she'd sucked on a lemon. "A dark arts practitioner or a dark witch."

A dark witch? They summoned demons. The odds of a black witch being responsible for raising the demon that marked Talia were high.

And now we needed their help?

In other words, we were screwed.

NINE

TALIA

Despite everything going on, Galen kept his word and left me on the rotation for watch duty. I looked forward to my shift each time. Not that I didn't enjoy my time with Max and looking after him, but I needed to get out of the house, to stretch my legs and let my wolf run.

I'd handled myself when Natasha showed up, kept my cool, and called for backup. I had even impressed David, Markus, and Theo—or the beta boys, as I liked to call them. Not to their face. I wasn't trying to get myself killed.

There were enough people trying to do that already.

David scheduled me for an additional watch, upping me to two per week. Which still left plenty of time for Max. And Galen.

Which would have been great, if he had been around to spend time with. Unfortunately, that wasn't the case.

At first, I tried not to take Galen's absence personally. After all, he was the alpha and alphas were busy. He was no exception, but I could tell it was more than that. Ever since Marguerite suggested contacting dark witches to remove the mark, he had pulled back emotionally and physically, and I saw him less and less.

He even started sleeping at his apartment in town above the bar, even though he'd closed his business weeks ago due to all the pack drama. But at least he couldn't avoid me when he came to see his father.

A few of the women in the pack stopped by the house to introduce themselves formally and invite me to be a member of the events committee. I was pretty sure that Julia, Samantha, and Michele *were* the events committee.

I was a little concerned that there was only three members but welcomed the distraction from the backslide in my relationship with Galen.

And the demon mark. Though that was a little harder to forget about since I had a physical reminder on my wrist of the demon's claim on my soul.

Today, I'd been nominated to make several batches of brownies for a pack picnic the committee had planned for the weekend. The idea was to boost pack morale with something pleasant to take everyone's mind off the lurking danger.

The event trio deserved some credit for how hard they worked to maintain a semblance of normal. With everything going on, a picnic was the furthest thing from my mind.

The oven announced it was ready for baking with three loud beeps that pulled me out of my thoughts and into the kitchen.

I slipped on my apron and set out the ingredients for the recipe. With everything premeasured and set aside, I set about mixing everything together. The baking dish went in the oven, and I repeated the process, measuring, mixing and baking until I was down to my last batch.

Galen strolled through the back door at that point, and snatched one of the individually wrapped brownies. "It smells delicious in here. You made all these?"

"I did." I yanked the bag from his hands and set it back on the counter. "They're for the picnic this weekend."

"Julia, Samantha, and Michele got their claws into you, I see."

Galen chuckled, snatched up another brownie I'd yet to wrap, and shoved half of it in his mouth before I could take it back.

His eyes widened with each chew until his eyebrows all but merged with his hairline.

When he could finally speak, he said, "This is the best brownie I've ever eaten. Are there mini chocolate chips in there?" He examined the inside of the remaining bit of brownie before he polished off the rest in one bite. "So good."

My heart swelled with pride at his pleasure in my baking skills, but I cleared my throat, trying not to care too much. The guy had been absent more than present recently, and I shouldn't have been getting so hung up on his approval. "I think I heard your dad." I dismissed him with a wave of my spatula.

I'd promised myself that I wouldn't hang around the house waiting for his visits with Max, just to be around him. If he wanted to pull back or slow down, then I needed to do the same.

My heart had suffered enough at Maddox's hands.

If I could spare myself any more heartache, I would.

"Thanks." Galen's shoulders slumped as he jogged across the kitchen. He stopped at the entrance to the living room and gripped the trim molding that ran along the opening. "I'm sorry."

"You don't have to apologi—"

"No, I do." He turned around and leaned against the jamb like he was shoring up the wall with his body. "I've had my hands full, and admittedly, I'm stretched a little thin, but I pulled back without any explanation to you."

"You don't owe me one. We aren't mated or anything." I set the spatula in the mixing bowl and wiped my hands on the front of my apron. "But I could do without the whiplash."

"You're right." He lowered his gaze and stared at the floor. "After Marguerite tried and failed to remove the mark—"

"Listen, if this is about working with dark witches, I'll understand if you don't want to. I can meet with them myself. It's fine."

"You say fine, which means it's definitely not fine." Galen met my gaze, a hint of humor in his eyes. "But that's not what freaked me out. It was the possibility of failing again, of not being able to fix this at all."

"Nobody is more scared of that than I am, but I don't have the option of hiding from it." I held up my arm and bared my mark. "I am constantly reminded about it."

"I know." He raked his fingers through his hair, tugging through a few tangles at the ends. "It's just, I've been through this type of thing before, and I couldn't save her. I backed off from you in an effort to save myself from more pain, but not being with you hurts."

"Galen, I don't need a hero. I need a friend. Someone I can count on, who isn't going to disappear on me when things don't go the way they planned. Life can be messy and painful, but I need someone who can be there for all of it. If you can't do that, I'll understand, but I need to know now."

I wasn't sure who was more surprised by my ultimatum—Galen or me. But it needed to be said. I was acutely aware of the fact that the demon mark might kill me. I didn't want to waste precious time on an emotional rollercoaster.

I wanted Galen to be my rock, but I wouldn't beg or force him.

"I can do that." He pushed off the wall and stalked toward me. "I *am* your friend, Talia. I won't bail on you again. I promise."

"Don't make a promise you don't intend to keep, Galen. I'm giving you an out. This is your chance to cut your losses and run." I leaned against the counter and crossed my arms over my chest.

Deep down inside, my wolf snarled. She didn't want Galen to run. She wanted him to stay close, and she was mad at me for giving him the chance to get away from us.

"I never make a promise I don't intend to keep." He pinched my chin between his thumb and forefinger and raised my head until I met his gaze. "And I am not going to run. I will stay right here, by your side, no matter what happens."

"It's about damn time you came to your senses," Max shouted from his bedroom. "Stubborn ass."

"Dad, stop eavesdropping," Galen fired back. "This was obviously a private conversation."

"There is no such thing as privacy with my shifter hearing and these paper-thin walls. Besides, I'm bed ridden. I need entertainment and you two are better than daytime TV."

"Keep it up, Max, and I won't bring you any of these brownies." I was not above threatening him with baked goods.

"Shutting up now." The old wolf didn't make a peep after that.

"Take him a brownie when you go see him, please." I reached for one of the brownies already packaged in a bag.

"I was thinking I could stay down here with you for a while." Galen sounded unsure of himself, as if he expected me to say no.

"I'm just going to be baking. It's fine. Go visit with your dad."

"You said fine again." One corner of his mouth curved up into a lopsided grin.

"This is one of those instances where fine actually does mean fine," I said, mirroring his smile.

"And how exactly does one know the difference?" he asked with a laugh, but I suspected he was only half-joking.

"These are girl club trade secrets, Galen. I'd be breaking several club rules if I told you." I twirled a lock of his luscious hair around my finger. "But if you promise not to share the secret with anyone else, including the beta boys, I'll tell you."

"The beta boys?" Galen busted out laughing. "Do they know you call them that?"

"Of course not." I gasped at my slip. I hadn't meant to say that out loud. "Despite what the universe seems to think, I don't have a death wish."

That made him laugh harder and I was glad his sense of humor had returned, at least around me. Everything had been life or death and there hadn't been much to laugh about.

But you had to find your joy where you could.

I was tired of crying.

"Man, I needed that." Galen coughed and wiped his eyes, pulling himself together. "How about I give you a hand with the rest of the brownies?"

"Do you even know how to bake?" I asked, unable to hide the skepticism in my voice.

Maddox had been useless in the kitchen and had zero inclination to improve. He'd been more into traditional roles when it came to tasks around the house.

"Of course." Galen slid the cookbook in front of him and sorted the ingredients. He mixed and measured with the ease of someone proficient in the kitchen.

"I'm impressed." I pulled out a chair from the kitchen table and sat back to watch him work.

There was something incredibly sexy about a man who knew his way around a kitchen.

I swooped in when he removed the bowl from the electric stand mixer and dragged my finger through the batter for a taste test. Galen grabbed my hand and wrapped his mouth around my finger down the knuckle, sucking it clean.

"Mm, delicious." He ran his tongue around the tip of my finger once more for good measure. "You'll just have to wait until they're ready."

"Okay." I wobbled back to my seat on suddenly jelly-like legs.

He poured the batter into a glass baking dish, slid it in the oven, and set a timer.

"Twenty minutes. How on earth will I pass the time?" He padded across the vinyl floor toward me with a look in his eye like a predator stalking its prey.

My senses immediately heightened, heat pooling between my legs, as it always did when Galen showed his desire for me.

He bent down and brought his lips close to mine but waited for me to close the distance and initiate the kiss. I ran my tongue along his lips, deepening the kiss when he opened his mouth to me.

The passion between us flared and for long minutes I lost myself in his delicious kiss, until Galen eventually pulled away. I almost whimpered a denial—until he grabbed me and hauled me close against his obviously aroused body.

I needed him, and soon. But now was not the time. Especially with his father only a room away. I allowed a moment longer to enjoy the hard heat of his flesh against my belly, then shot him a wry grin and shook my head.

"How about a movie?" I wanted to make love to Galen, but my first time was not going to be on a kitchen table, with an audience listening in from the next room.

He sighed as if hard done by, and leaned forward to kiss my lips softly. His expression said he knew why I'd stopped, and reluctantly agreed. "Sounds like a plan."

The brownies were done and we were curled up on the couch with a bowl of popcorn and an old monster movie marathon playing on the TV when Galen got a call.

"It's one of the beta boys," he said as he picked up his cell.

His snicker at the nickname I'd come up with was cut short when David shouted on the other end of the phone about a full-fledged attack from the Northwood pack. We could hear growling and snarling in the background.

Both Galen and I jumped to our feet.

Fucking assholes never quit.

The wards near the main entrance to the pack lands were down, and several wolves had been injured.

I shoved the bowl of popcorn onto the coffee table and shut off the TV.

Galen was already in the kitchen searching for his keys. We could run of course, but we'd get to the pack's border a lot faster in Galen's truck. And that way, we could conserve our shifter energy for fighting, if we needed to.

"Let's go." Galen said brusquely.

Galen pulled the truck forward, cut the wheel hard to the left, and hit the gas. We tore through the grass, over the sidewalk, and bounced off the curb into the street.

We pulled up near the perimeter of the pack's land in record time. There, the fight was still in full swing. Teeth were bared, and a blur of fur and teeth were everywhere as growling, snarling wolves of all colors and sizes ripped into each other.

Galen's wolf burst free of his skin the moment he was out of the car. He disappeared into the fray. I was right behind him, my wolf almost jumping out of my skin in her eagerness to be free. The Northwood pack had Galen's pack outnumbered, but not over-powered.

Maddox and his father generally filled their ranks with weaker wolves to ensure they weren't challenged and held on to the seat of power.

Galen's strategy was the opposite. He was confident in his own ability to hold leadership, and therefore welcomed strong wolves and independent thinkers. His pack was better for it. Especially in a situation like this.

Galen's wolves rallied when they saw him, and fell into formation. They attacked as a group and tore through wolf after wolf from the Northwood pack.

Maddox howled, calling for his men to retreat. He left the wounded for Galen to deal with. It looked like the meeting house would serve yet another function besides a prison—emergency room.

A lesser alpha would have left the enemy wolves in the field to fend for themselves. Or killed them once and for all.

But not Galen.

His good nature and leadership based on morality were just a couple of the things I loved about him.

Even in the midst of the fight, the word love gave me pause.

After years of associating the word with Maddox, it felt strange to think it in the same sentence as another wolf. But there wasn't another word in the English language to describe the feelings I had for Galen. I *was* falling in love with him.

I made a promise to myself to tell him how I felt if the demon mark was able to be removed.

But that was a really big *if*.

CHAPTER

TEN

GALEN

The Northwood pack had obviously figured out a way to break the wards, which had rattled me more than I would admit.

Marguerite and her coven had their work cut out to repair the damage Maddox had done to the magical protections placed around the property. The witch wasn't sure how he'd done it, but she suspected dark witches and equally dark magic were involved.

Dark magic was to blame for a lot of our problems, it seemed. And yet, we needed the help of the dark witches to have any chance of removing Talia's demon mark. It seemed the universe was not without a sense of irony.

Talia and I brought food and magical supplies to the witches who were working around the clock to rebuild their barriers. David, Markus, and Theo volunteered to help with the wounded. By the end of the battle, the Northwood injured members had outnumbered our own.

We'd patched them up and our prisoners were now resting in the warded cabin in which I'd once kept Talia. Theo was on watch, but they couldn't escape. Not even if they were physically able to.

To my relief, the rest of the day had been uneventful. Once

89

Maddox and his followers had retreated there had been no further signs of the Northwood pack, or their dark witch friends.

The next day was the day of the picnic and despite everything going on, I decided to allow it to go ahead. The pack needed something positive to enjoy at the present time.

I'd considered canceling the event, but in fact it was Talia who convinced me it would be good for the pack to come together. Even something as simple as a pack picnic might lift morale.

She was right, of course.

Julia, Samantha, and Michele had roped Talia into helping and she'd baked enough brownies to feed an army. We swung by Dad's house, loaded the trays of brownies into the back seat and tray of the truck, then headed over to the pasture.

I assumed that most of the pack members wouldn't attend; that they would prefer to tend to their wounds. Or just stay home for peace and quiet. But when we parked under a tree and I looked out the window, every wolf who was able to attend was there with blankets and casserole dishes in hand.

"What a turnout," Talia said with a grin.

I nodded, grinning back at her. "Better than expected. Let's go." We jumped out of the truck and started unloading. The picnic became a potluck. Talia and I dropped the brownies off at the dessert table and found an empty patch of grass in the middle of the field. She spread a blanket out for us to share and then dragged me into the line for food. We piled fried chicken and spoonfuls of every kind of salad known to man or wolf onto our plates.

The food was delicious and for the first time in too long, I felt like I could take a breath.

With so many attacks and the demons destroying the town, it amazed me that I hadn't been challenged for alpha yet.

Emphasis on *yet*. It felt inevitable somehow. But for the time being, it seemed I had the support of my pack. And that was enough.

Despite the way Talia had found her way into our pack, she now fitted in just as well as anyone else.

When we'd finished eating, I lay back on the blanket. Talia groaned and rubbed her stomach. "Now I know what a Thanksgiving turkey feels like."

"A Thanksgiving turkey?" I stopped cloud-watching and rolled my head to look at her.

"Yeah, you know, stuffed." She giggled. "Oh, I shouldn't laugh. My stomach hurts when I laugh."

"Do you want me to rustle up some antacids?" I propped myself up on my elbows. "Michele probably has some in that Mary Poppins bag of hers. She's got everything else in there."

"She's kind of a den mother, huh?" Talia watched a group of kids running around the field playing a game of tag.

"Yeah, I think it just happens naturally after you've raised six kids." I lay back down, tucking my hands under my head. "With her kids grown, she's pretty much just adopted everyone in the pack."

"She's sweet." Talia laid down and curled up beside me, resting her head in the crook of my shoulder. One of her hands curved possessively on my chest, and I found that I liked it. I placed my hand over hers, keeping it there.

"That she is."

The sun on my face and the warmth from Talia's body pressed against mine lulled me into a much-needed nap.

We'd invited Marguerite and her witches to join us if and when they could. She agreed to send them in shifts so that they could rest and recharge.

When I woke, Talia sat up and rubbed her eyes. She'd obviously been sleeping too.

"Oh, there's Sarah." she said, pointing to the young witch she'd made friends with.

"Oh hi, you two." A weary smile fleetingly appeared on Sarah's abnormally pale face.

"You okay?" I asked her.

She put her hand up to her forehead as if she had a headache, and swayed where she stood. "Yeah, I'm okay. I just... I'm a bit tired. That's all."

Talia met my gaze and suddenly seemed as worried as I was.

She jumped to her feet and took Sarah over to the table to get some food. But there was something off about the witch, and whatever it was couldn't be fixed with anything we were serving at the buffet.

She barely touched the food. Talia set Sarah up on a chair a few feet away from our blanket, and then hurried over to whisper to me. "I think we need to call Marguerite."

"We need to do more than that." I got up and dusted off my hands, concern churning in my gut. "We need to search for the goddamn demon. She's cursed, isn't she?"

"I think so." Talia frowned and nibbled at her lip. "I'll call Marguerite. You find David." She already had her phone wedged between her ear and shoulder.

I spotted David walking away from the dessert table with a plate piled high with baked goods and called out to him. He turned, half a brownie protruding from his mouth, and waved. I pointed to Sarah, who'd gotten out of her chair and was now staggering through the field in a haphazard manner.

"What in the actual..." He dropped his plate and rushed over to me.

"I guess one day of solace was too much to ask." I slipped an elastic tie off my wrist and secured my hair back out of the way. "She's cursed."

"I'm starting to think we all are."

Neither of us laughed. There was some truth to David's joke.

All things considered, the idea that the pack had been cursed wasn't an unreasonable conclusion. It made more sense than anything I could come up with for all the crap we'd dealt with lately.

"You keep an eye on her. I'll get Marguerite."

David nodded and followed Sarah around the pasture. She wasn't really doing anything wrong, but she looked unwell.

Talia rushed up to me. "Marguerite's on her way."

Some of my pack members were staring at me now, concern written in the lines of their face. I smiled and waved, wanting them to continue to enjoy the day while they could.

It wasn't their fault that I couldn't go an hour without thinking of the demons that plagued us, or the wolves that wanted us dead so they could take our land.

We waited for Marguerite to arrive and, when she did, she came with three other witches.

"Where is she?" Marguerite asked.

I pointed toward the food tables where Sarah was now pushing David away from her. "Over there. She is not herself."

Marguerite sighed. "Half my coven is under the influence. That's the real reason I couldn't send most of them here for the picnic. They're under house arrest."

I groaned and ran my hand through my hair. "It's the demons, isn't it?"

She nodded. "I don't know how my witches became infected, but I'm doing my best to keep them safe until the effects wear off."

I crossed my arms over my chest. "I appreciate that, thanks." The witches who'd gone insane in town due to demon influence had turned the whole place upside down.

"I'll take Sarah back and lock her in her tent."

I watched Marguerite gather Sarah up, and the coven members left.

The rest of my pack at the picnic seemed to immediately relax, which made guilt settle even heavier in my chest. I'd been the one to say the witches could stay. I'd offered sanctuary, hoping the demons wouldn't be able to find them here.

"What do you wanna do now?" Talia asked, the pleasure of the picnic forgotten.

David strolled over to join the conversation.

"I want to find the demon that has influenced the witches," I said, stripping off my shirt. "It has to be nearby to be affecting the coven like that."

David nodded. "I'll join you."

"I'll stay and keep an eye on everyone here," Talia said. "Unless you'd prefer that I join you?"

I shook my head. "No. Stay, please. I'll meet you back home in a few hours."

I caught her beautiful smile before I let go of my humanity and shifted. David joined me in wolf form and we went in search of the demon.

David and I ran the property line together, taking extra care to check out the areas that had known weaknesses remaining in the wards. There were a lot.

Less than half of the wards had been rebuilt and it was unlikely any more repairs would be made if the witches were being influenced by a demon running lose on pack land. They needed every ounce of their magic to protect themselves until we found the creature.

And that wasn't looking good.

We ran the length of the property again with Markus and Theo, then Markus split his group of twelve wolves into four smaller groups and marked off quadrants for each group to search more thoroughly.

There was no sign of the demon anywhere.

If I hadn't seen the cursed witch for myself, I wouldn't have believed a demon had made it onto the property.

I found it hard to believe the demon had cursed a few of them and left. The demons in town cursed as many witches as they could find. He wouldn't have had to look very hard.

There were plenty of witches on the property.

Hours went by and we came up empty-handed. There was no scent trail to follow or physical sign of a demon's presence anywhere. It was as if the demon had done his dirty work on the witches, then vanished into thin air.

We couldn't go on like this, especially without the safety of the wards. The pack and the coven were vulnerable.

I had to do something.

I shifted not far from the coven's area and spoke to my protective detail of wolves. "Go home those of you who aren't on night duty, and get some rest. I'm going to speak to Marguerite."

They headed off and I ducked into one of the bachelor cabins and grabbed a pair of jeans. Most of the pack wouldn't care if I turned up for a meeting naked.

The witches would.

When I knocked on Marguerite's small cabin, she opened the door immediately. "Did you find anything?"

I shook my head. "Nothing."

"Shit." She groaned, putting both hands on her hips as though she were pissed off at my incompetence.

"I agree." I took a deep breath. "So, despite the fact that this goes against everything I believe, would you please set up a meeting with a dark witch?"

Marguerite's eyes widened. "Are you sure? I know it's not what you want to do."

I nodded. "Yes I'm sure. Desperate times call for desperate measures. And this is becoming desperate times."

And if Marguerite was right, the dark witch may be able to help Talia as well as the pack.

ELEVEN

GALEN

Contrary to popular belief, wolf shifters are not immortal, just hard to kill—unless you're a crazed witch armed with tainted and powerful magic.

That seemed to be enough to level the playing field.

The demon's curse spread through the coven like wildfire. More and more witches became infected, and two had been crazed enough to attack members of our pack. They used magic to snap bones and cause massive internal injuries.

Luckily, the wolves who'd been attacked survived.

Unluckily for the witches, those attacks didn't end well for them. My wolves retaliated and killed them both.

It was horrible, and the unease that had existed between the wolves and witches grew into outright hatred.

My pack had been under attack from the Northwood pack for weeks before the demons began to intensify everything. When the witches I'd let into our pack began to attack us as well, from the inside it felt like, that was the last straw.

My alliance with Marguerite and her coven hung by a thread after the two witches were slain. It hadn't mattered to most of the coven that the deaths were the result of self-defense and an unpro-voked attack by insane, demon-cursed witches.

A dead witch was a dead witch in their view, and that fueled anger on both sides.

I couldn't help but wonder if their reaction had something to do with their affliction. If they hadn't all been affected by a demon curse to some degree, would they have been more understanding?

I liked to think so.

At least where Marguerite was concerned. She was a levelheaded and practical witch. I *liked* her. Surely, she couldn't expect my wolves not to defend themselves when attacked. Even if the attacker was under the influence of a demon curse.

I spent the morning as I had done for days now, running the perimeter, grateful the witches still unaffected by the curse had agreed to continue their work on repairing the wards after the pack retaliated against their sisters. There was still no proof that the demons had breached the property line. So how did they get in?

Something told me that when I found my answer, I'd find one for Talia, too. All our problems were connected, and I had a terrible feeling her mark was at the center of everything.

Running in wolf form was the only thing that took my mind off Talia's demon mark, so I picked up extra shifts on watch throughout the week.

Tonight, the full moon was covered by clouds, but I felt her silvery pull just the same. My wolf shifter ran faster, around a tree and into the field where the picnic had been held. It hadn't been that long ago, but it felt like a lifetime.

And yet, tonight, in the light of the moon, my heart lifted. What a magnificent evening!

I raised my snout and sniffed the fresh breeze as I trotted forward across the grass, then quickly lowered it again when I caught the scent of something not of nature.

Out of the corner of my eye, I saw something move. I turned to see a witch charging across the open field, her long blond hair flying behind her like a long ribbon in the wind.

My instincts sent a growl of unease through my chest and I skidded to a halt, hoping to stay out of her way. But she wasn't trying to avoid me. Quite the opposite.

She blasted me with a bolt of magic that sent me tumbling ass over tail. She raised her hand and fired again. *Fuck!* I rolled to the right and narrowly missed getting shot in my hind quarters.

When I had all four paws on the ground I ran for it, cutting across the field in a zigzag pattern. As I hoped, it proved harder for her to hit a moving target. Somehow, I needed to circle back and subdue the witch without killing her.

Easier said than done when my best defenses were sharp teeth and claws.

Still, Marguerite and her coven would not forgive any more casualties and we needed their help as much as they needed ours.

Even with the witch affliction reaching the pack lands, less witches had been infected here than in town. We hadn't seen signs of another demon. The same couldn't be said for anyone living in town.

I couldn't afford to make a mistake and hurt the witch hurling magical balls of death at me from behind.

Shit. Shit. Think. Think. What do I do?

I had to wear her down and lure her back to the coven encampment and Marguerite. It was a good plan, but it had one tiny flaw.

She needed to follow me.

The witch didn't seem to be all that interested in chasing me any longer. She wasn't running after me, and she was staring off into the distance in the direction of the town.

Fuck. Why would she chase me when there were wolves all over the property that she could attack—probably more easily than me? Unfortunately for her, they would attack back.

I tapped into the pack bond and sent word for any wolf on pack lands to take shelter, and to hold off entering the picnic field unless they were scheduled for a security detail. I was setting a trap and didn't need one of my wolves inadvertently becoming the bait.

When there were no other wolves within sight for her to attack, she turned and glared at me, then began to follow me again. I didn't hit my full stride, wanting to ensure she kept up. But that proved to be a mistake. It turned out witches were faster than I expected. Or at least, this one was.

She ran up beside me, leapt onto my back, and grabbed fistfuls of fur. Pain ripped into my flesh and I tried to shake her off, but she dug her heels into my side and held on.

She twisted her fingers deeper into my fur until she touched skin and lit me up with a lightning spell. Every cell in my body was in pain.

I collapsed to the ground, writhing in pain with her still on top of me.

Oh my God...

I'd underestimated my opponent. That could be the last mistake I ever made.

The witch leapt to her feet, brushing the dirt and grass from her clothes. She lifted her arms and wriggled her fingers, clearly readying herself for another spell. I tried to get up, but my legs shook and I couldn't get my paws under me.

The lightning bolts she conjured sizzled in her hands, but instead of shooting them out and killing me straight away, she held them for a moment at her fingertips.

I'd made an error earlier. Now, so had she.

I wasn't going to lie here and let her kill me. I seized the opportunity and launched at her, clamping down on her forearm and sinking my teeth into her flesh. I didn't want to kill her, but she'd survive one bite.

The lightning fizzled out and she screeched in pain. At the first tang of coppery blood on my tongue, I released her arm.

I gathered enough strength to make a final run for the coven, got to my still-shaking legs and took off. She howled and raced after me, but I wasn't going to let her grab me this time. I put everything I had into this run. My heart pounded and pain screamed in every part of my body, begging me to stop.

You stop and you'll die. Just keep moving.

As we reached the encampment, the witch fired multiple shots in my direction. I kept running, weaving through the tents scattered about the grounds.

The tent flaps opened and when I finally reached the cabin where Marguerite lived, her door opened and she rushed out just as I collapsed on the porch steps.

The woman ran toward us. Marguerite stood in front of me, putting herself between me and the crazed witch.

Lighting magic shot our way, but Marguerite put up her hands, creating some sort of magical shield. The rest of the coven who'd appeared from various tents grabbed the blond witch and held her down.

She screamed like a banshee, writhing and fighting against their braced arms. Sarah raced out of her house and joined them, holding a large potion bottle.

Marguerite took the potion bottle and chanted in a language I didn't recognize while she poured the purple potion over the blond witch's face. The woman, who'd moments ago been dead set on killing me, stopped screaming, then passed out, collapsing in the arms of one of her coven members.

Marguerite ran her hand through the blond witch's hair, spoke to the others, and they carried her away.

I gaped at the high priestess. What was she doing? Sedating her witch? Or curing her? That was beyond her abilities, surely?

I shifted back, wanting out of my pain-wracked body, and needing my vocal cords back.

My human body came back to me, but the pain was still there. Not as bad, but damn...

I shuddered as I got to my feet and stretched out my back, hoping to be able to soothe some of the quivering muscles.

Sarah came over to me, a pair of jeans in her hand. She glanced away. "I, ah... conjured these for you."

"Thanks," I said, grabbing the jeans and managing to slide my aching legs into the pants, before collapsing to sit on the steps once more. "Fuck... that hurt."

Sarah twisted around to stare at me. "She got you?"

I nodded. "Oh yeah."

"I'll be right back." She raced off into her cabin, then came back a few moments later with a small vial of red liquid.

"This is for the pain," she said. "It should help."

I didn't even ask what was in it. I just tossed it back, wincing at the strangely grass-like flavor.

Immediately, the pain of the lightning attack began to subside. I groaned with relief and sunk deeper down on the stairs. "Thank you. That's heaps better."

Marguerite had gone with the witches to put the blond somewhere, so I took a minute to get my breath back. I'd made it without killing the witch, and everyone had seen me show restraint. Hopefully that would help to repair some of the rift between the pack and the coven.

"So, you're feeling better then?" Last time I'd seen Sarah, she'd been under the effects of the curse, too.

"Marguerite managed to stave it off before it fully took hold," she said. Then she shuddered. "Thank the goddess."

I opened my mouth to ask more when I heard a shout.

"Galen!"

It was Talia. I sat up to look for her. She ran over to me and I got to my feet. She wrapped her arms around me, enveloping me in a hug. "You're okay. I was so worried."

I hugged her back, tightly, enjoying the connection. There had been several moments when I'd worried I'd never be able to hold her again, so the relief pulsing through me now was a palpable thing. "How did you even know what happened?"

Sarah inched her hand up in the air, a sheepish smile on her face. I should have known.

It suddenly occurred me that Talia wasn't pack. She wouldn't have gotten the message to steer clear of the field. She'd integrated so seamlessly into my life and the daily life of the pack, I'd forgotten nothing had been made official.

And that oversight could have cost Talia her life. We needed to rectify that, and soon.

I pulled back from her hug and grinned down on her. "You didn't have to rush out here. I'm fine. Not a scratch on me."

It was a slight exaggeration, but she didn't need to know that. I hugged her again, harder than usual, until she *oomphed* and said I was squeezing the air out of her lungs.

"But I'm happy to see you." I released my hold slightly.

She tapped my shoulder blade and sucked in a deep breath. "I can see that."

Marguerite exited the tent where they'd taken the crazed witch, then walked over to us. "I want to thank you, Galen."

"There's nothing to thank me for, Marguerite." I let go of Talia and shook the witch's proffered hand. "I don't want any harm to come to your witches or my wolves."

The coven hadn't needed an infirmary until the Northwood pack brought the wards down and let a demon in. Maddox would pay for what happened to the coven and to my pack. I planned to see to it personally.

"Galen." Marguerite rested her left hand on my shoulder and squeezed, pulling me from my thoughts. "We've tried everything at our disposal and can't stop this curse from spreading. Like with Sarah, if we get to the witch early enough, we can help stop it. But mostly it's too late by the time we realize someone has been affected. Perhaps if we had access to more of our gardens and root cellars we left behind, but even then, I'm not sure."

"I'm sorry so many of your sisters have been afflicted." I covered her hand with mine. "I'm not sure what, if anything, we can do, but you know I'm here for you and yours."

"You may very well regret that offer, Galen, because there *is* something you can do for us." The fine lines at the corners of her eyes and around her mouth deepened.

The stress had taken a physical toll on the high priestess.

I knew how she felt. It had worn me down as well. We all needed a break but there was no relief in sight that I could see.

"Let's hope I don't regret it." I released her hand and crossed my arms over my chest. "What do you need?"

"As I said, we can't conjure a cure for the curse once it takes hold, but I know of a coven that might. In Jarrettsville." Marguerite tucked an errant strand of her silver hair behind her ear.

"Another coven?" I shook my head. "No offense, but that sounds like a witch thing to me. Wouldn't it be better if someone from your coven reached out to the other coven?"

"We would, Galen." Marguerite steepled her hands in front of her mouth and inhaled a deep breath. "But we're forbidden to deal with them."

"Now I'm really confused. So, you can't make deals with this other coven, whoever they are, but you want me to ask them to help you?"

"Precisely. I need you to buy a potion from them. I'll give you all the details." She spoke as if that cleared up everything.

It didn't.

"It might help if we knew why you can't work with these witch-es," Talia said, prodding for more information.

At least I wasn't the only one who struggled to follow Marguerite's logic.

"Isn't it obvious?" Marguerite let out an exasperated sigh when she took in our baffled expressions. "They dabble in the dark arts."

"So, they're dark witches." Talia perked up at that bit of knowl-edge. "That's a good thing! They might know how to get rid of my mark."

"They're more in the gray area. I wouldn't expect them to know anything about summoning demons, but the magic they do practice crosses a line my coven will not." Marguerite turned her nose up over the other witches' preferred method of magic.

It seemed pretentious of her, considering her magic had failed to save her coven or Talia. She was too good to wield the magic, but she wasn't above using a potion that was a result of that magic.

A bit of a contradiction.

Not that I was in a position to judge. Talia and I needed help from even darker witches than the ones Marguerite wanted us to buy a cure from.

"I guess we're going on a road trip," I said to Talia, whose eyes lit up at the request.

Talia needed a cure, and so did Marguerite.

CHAPTER

TWELVE

TALIA

Dark magic had gone from being our last resort to our next best hope. I wasn't sure what that said about our chances, but it couldn't have been anything good.

Marguerite sent us on a mission behind enemy lines to make a deal with a coven that didn't just walk the line between good and evil; they danced right over it according to Sarah.

Magic was still a bit of a mystery to me, but I'd learned more about its mechanics thanks to Sarah and Marguerite. Prior to Galen taking in the coven, I hadn't had the opportunity to meet many witches, never mind learn about their magic.

I supposed that was something positive to come from being demon marked. The witches were inadvertently teaching me their craft as they researched ways to remove the mark. I wouldn't be able to wield magic because I wasn't born with that spark that made a person a witch, but it gave me a greater appreciation for who they were and a deeper connection to nature.

When we left pack grounds and drove through the nearby town where Galen's bar was situated, I hardly recognized the historic district. Stores had been looted and burned. Windows were boarded.

Trash littered the ground and blew across the street like tumbleweeds.

The only people on the streets seemed to be afflicted witches whostumbled along the sidewalks, bumping into lampposts and benches, like a horde of zombies.

There wasn't a mortal person in sight.

"Oh my God, Galen. It's so much worse than I realized."

He sighed. "Yeah. There's a reason I closed the bar, and it wasn't just the pack wars."

Galen slowed the truck to a crawl and took care not to rev the engine or hit any debris in the road. We didn't want to draw the attention of the cursed witches. They seemed to be a in a stupor, as if they were sleepwalking without anything left to attack.

We preferred not to make a target of ourselves.

The truck offered some protection, but Galen and I had seen cursed witches in action. The demons seemed to be able to make the witches' innate magic darker and more powerful. It was as if the curse enhanced and tainted their magic at the same time.

After seeing what was left of the town, I felt better about the choices we'd been forced to make in relation to taking in the witches and protecting ourselves with wards.

"Do you see any demons?" I looked away from the devastation outside my window and turned my attention to Galen.

"Just the aftermath." He gripped the steering wheel with his left hand and curled his right into a fist in his lap.

I put my hand to the window, wanting to heal the pain of the town and its people. "The witches have their work cut out for them when this is all over."

The shops on the opposite side of the street hadn't fared any better. It was a disaster area.

"We all have our work cut out." Galen spoke in clipped tones, but I knew his anger wasn't directed at me. "This is the pack's town as much as it is anyone else's. We've been supporting this whole area for years and we have a responsibility to the humans who live here to help fix it."

My heart went out to Galen. He was an alpha to his very core, wanting to help anyone weaker than himself. Which, given his strength, was pretty much everyone.

He also owned a business and home in this town. Surely it upset him to see that go to ruin as well? I wasn't sure he was up to me asking questions about it though, so I kept my comments vague. "I think it's admirable that you and your pack have devoted so much of yourselves to supporting the community. The Northwood pack only cared about themselves. It was never about doing good, only what they could get."

"Maddox and his father give wolves everywhere a bad name. They'll get what's coming to them, Talia. I promise." Galen eased the truck into a lefthand turn and slowly accelerated when we reached the edge of town.

"Hey, can we chat about something else for a sec?" His tone indicated that this was going to be a serious conversation.

I twisted in my seat to look at him. "Of course. What's up?' It had to be about the pack, or us, or his dad, or the witches. Or even the demons, or my mark. Shit, we had a lot going on.

"David and I are in the process of drafting a challenge request to the Northwood alpha. We wanted to take our time, make sure we cover every scenario and leave no room for error—no loopholes they can wriggle out of."

I swallowed hard against the sudden lump in my throat. "Ah... okay." I didn't know what else to say. That hadn't been on my list of things to worry about at the moment.

Galen glanced my way. "I vow to end Maddox and his father's reign over the Northwood pack, Talia. And, given your past, I want your blessing to do so."

I relaxed back into my seat and stared out the windscreen for a minute, needing to think. "You know I want to take them down myself, Galen. I want vengeance for my father. For me. For the life they stole. For *everything* bad they've done."

Even though I now knew that I would have been miserable married to Maddox, the damage that they'd done to me needed acknowledgment.

"I know. But the last time you spoke of your need for vengeance, you passed out."

I sighed. "That's true." I hadn't forgotten I'd been so angry that my mark had burned and sent me into a short-time coma.

"So, would you leave the challenge to me? At least... to begin with?"

I bit my lip, thinking quickly. "I love that you want to do this, for me, and for the pack. But..." I trailed off.

Galen was an alpha. If anyone could beat my old fiancé and his father, it was Galen.

"Look, I understand your need for vengeance, I have it too," he said. "And I know you're one of the smartest, strongest, and most capable wolves I've met, Talia. But the Northwoods never fight fair, and I can't lose you."

His words made my heart sing and squeeze tight all at once.

"I can't lose you either," I choked out.

He reached out and squeezed my thigh. The touch sent heat right through me. "But you'll let me send the challenge?"

I nodded and gulped out, "Okay. Yes."

"Thank you." His tone wasn't triumphant, or gloating. It was respectful. Suddenly, I knew it was the right decision to let Galen do this. I didn't want to be hurt, or upset about this. If anything, I was proud of the fact Galen was willing and able to fight on our behalf.

But I also knew that I wanted to be there, fighting alongside him. This challenge wouldn't be one-on-one if I could help it.

We were silent for a while and I went back to staring out the window once the scenery changed to trees with canopies of gold and burnt orange leaves. "How far is it to the town where the dark coven is?"

"About an hour. Why, you have somewhere to be after this?" Galen chuckled and spared a glance in my direction.

"Yeah, I am super busy. I mean, my calendar is so full." I smiled alongside him.

We passed the time with a you-laugh-you-lose challenge, telling each other bad dad jokes to see who would laugh first. Losing had never been so much fun. My stomach and sides hurt by the time we cruised into the dark coven's town.

It looked a lot like ours.

I don't know what I'd expected. Some sort of Halloween town or goth revival, maybe, but nothing was painted black or decorated with bats and spiders.

Nothing screamed welcome to Jarrettsville, home to dark witches, circa eighteen-seventy-three.

"Did Marguerite say how we were supposed to find the coven once we got here?" I marveled at the similarities of this little town to ours, but the major difference was glaring.

These shops and residences remained untouched by crazy cursed witches.

"We don't find them. They find us." Galen pulled the truck into a parking space and turned the key, powering down the engine.

"That sounds ominous." I was only half kidding.

"Looks like the coffee shop is open. I could use a cup right about now. You want anything?" Galen reached into the console and retrieved his wallet. He slid it into his back pocket as he stepped out of the truck.

"A latte sounds amazing. I'll come in with you." I hopped out of the truck and followed him into the cafe.

On the surface, it appeared to be a normal coffee house with espresso machines brewing and frothing in the background. Bakery cases filled with muffins and cakes led the flow of traffic toward the cashier waiting behind the counter.

But when I looked a little harder, I started to notice things.

Things like the drink selection: poisoned apple cider or the jack-o-latte. The day's special was soup bubbling away in a cauldron.

"Did we just get played by a bunch of witches?" Galen turned and looked at the décor. It had shifted from a retro diner with checkered floors and red booths, to haunted mansion with black walls and purple chairs.

"Maybe. This is weird, Galen. I was wondering what a town that dark witches lived in would look like and pictured sort of a Halloween vibe, you know?"

"A bit stereotypical, don't you think?" Galen bent down and examined the desserts in the glass cases.

"Yes, but I don't think that's really important right now." I crossed my arms over my chest and tapped my foot on the now black-tiled floor. "Do you?"

"Not at all." Galen straightened, turning toward me with a smile on his face. "Okay, so what do you think is going on right now? The coven is messing with you?"

"Yeah, I think so."

"But they'd need to have a mind reader to do that, right? You didn't say anything about it out loud until just now. So, the coven would have to have a powerful psychic to know what you were thinking." Galen took my hands in his and laced our fingers together. "I don't think—"

"It's not psychic ability," a young female voice said from the back of the coffee shop. "Just a little spell we crafted to read the intentions of people coming into our town here."

I squinted toward the back of the shop where the voice had come from, but couldn't see anyone.

Galen appeared to ignore the weirdness of the situation and said, "Please tell me there's still coffee here." Galen looked over at the espresso machine like it was a long-lost lover.

"Galen," I chastised. "Now probably isn't the time."

"I know, I know. It's just been a really long month and I could use the caffeine."

It was hard to argue with that.

A woman emerged from the shadows and walked toward us. "So, the old crone sent you?"

The witch looked to be in her late teens with short platinum blond hair tipped with indigo blue ends. So far, nothing about the town or its inhabitants was what I expected.

"You mean, Marguerite?" Galen leaned against the bakery case with his arms crossed over his chest.

He'd given up on his quest for caffeine and was back in business mode.

Marguerite had long silver hair and a few fine lines around her eyes, but she hardly qualified as an old crone in my opinion.

"That would be the old lady I was referring to, yes." The young witch slipped a black knit hat on her head, leaving just the blue bits of her hair exposed.

"What do you know about the demon curse that's afflicting the witches in town?" I asked, hoping to get the ball rolling.

"You're going to have to talk to Angelique." The young witch motioned for us to follow her. "I'm just the welcoming committee."

"I feel really welcomed, don't you?" Galen muttered.

"I lifted the glamour and let you inside, didn't I?" The witch led us down a narrow hall and out the back door. "We may not be shifters, but our hearing is pretty good."

I gave Galen a side-eyed glare and silent warning to curb his atti-tude. He raised his hands in a placating gesture.

"I'm sorry," he said to the witch. "I get abrasive when I'm exhausted. But that's no excuse for being rude."

"It doesn't bother me, but I would be on your best behavior with Angelique. She's not as warm and fuzzy as I am."

I'd met old wool blankets warmer and fuzzier than our escort, but I kept that comment to myself. No need to offend her again.

We followed her down an alleyway that ran parallel to the stores that lined the main street through town. There were metal doors on the left side, each stamped in white paint with the store name.

Matching aluminum trashcans were set on the left side of each door and a large dumpster sat on the far end of the back alley.

The witch turned right out of the alley and onto a residential street dotted with brick ranch-style homes and a couple of small two-story homes with dormer windows and screened-in front porches. It reminded me of my old neighborhood.

I looked at Galen, arching a brow. He seemed to pick up on my train of thought because he nodded and mouth the word, *weird*.

It was like a carbon copy of our town.

Except for the old Victorian house that sat on the corner lot.

We didn't have one of those and I assumed that it was the home of their high priestess.

"Is that Angelique's house?" I pointed to the massive black and white three story with scalloped wooden siding and clay-tiled roof.

"What gave it away?" The young witch had the angsty teenager routine down pat, but I suspected she was older than she looked and acted.

"Just a good guess." I barely contained my eye roll.

We weren't off to a great start, and I hoped things would improve when we met Angelique. The witches back home were running out of time.

The young witch opened the gate in the hip-high white picket fence that surrounded the property. The front yard had herb gardens on either side of a concrete walkway that led up to an expansive front porch.

She pressed the doorbell and the front door creaked open, revealing a grand foyer with a Tiffany chandelier swaying from the ceiling.

I felt like I'd stepped back in time. Everything was matched to the period the house would have been built.

"Bring them in, Aubrey." A woman's gentle-toned voice carried out into the foyer from a parlor off to the left.

"Well, don't keep her waiting." Aubrey ushered us into the living room with a flap of her hands.

My wolf growled inside of me as my heart began to pound. We had little defenses against witches and here we were, just walking into the lion's den.

Galen slipped his hand into mine and interlinked our fingers. We shared a single, worried look for a moment, before following Aubrey's request, and walked into the large sitting room.

I wasn't sure what I was expecting, but a beautiful woman in a flowing white dress was not it. She was sitting on an elegant lounge, glasses perched on the edge of her nose as she stared at us.

There wasn't a witchy thing in sight. Just a huge book case and luxurious rugs and cushions.

Now that she'd dropped us off in front of the high priestess, Aubrey made her exit through a doorway on the opposite side of the room.

"I have to say, I'm disappointed my sister didn't come and speak with me herself," the high priestess said, her tone all honey and sugar.

I gaped at her. *Oh my God.* Angelique was just a younger version of Marguerite. Gorgeous long hair, and the same blue eyes.

Our visit to dark coven territory just got weirder and weirder.

"I'm sorry, did you say your sister?" Galen sounded as mystified by her statement as I was.

"She didn't tell you?" Angelique steepled her fingers in front of her face, the gesture oddly familiar. "I'm not surprised. She wrote me off years ago. I told her not to be so judgmental, that she might need my help one day. And here we are."

"So, you know about the curse, then?" I felt a glimmer of hope rise within me. "Can you help us?"

If she knew about the demons plaguing our town, and had a cure for their influence, maybe she could remove my demon mark too.

"Of course, I know about the curse. Unlike my sister, I make it my business to know what is happening in the towns around my own. Things like this have a tendency to spread, and I don't want my coven members affected by any demons."

Marguerite had told us at least one truth about the coven before she sent us out here. If Angelique didn't want her witches tainted with the demon affliction, she wouldn't have condoned calling them. Angelique's coven wasn't as dark as I'd hoped.

It was a strange sort of disappointment. As much as I didn't want to be in the same room with a full-fledged dark witch, according to Marguerite, I might need one to remove the mark.

Angelique was the coven's best chance at a cure, but she probably wasn't the witch *I* was looking for.

The mark on my wrist itched in response to my thoughts about having it removed. It was becoming more sentient and in tune with my emotions. And that meant the demon who marked me was, too.

Marguerite and her coven weren't the only ones on a clock. I was, as well, and it was ticking down.

I lifted my chin, determined to get things moving. "Marguerite hasn't been able to conjure a potion strong enough to lift the curse once it takes hold. She can contain it to an extent, but not cure it."

I wasn't sure if Marguerite wanted me to share that little piece of information with her estranged sister, but honesty seemed like the best policy if we had any chance of leaving here with a cure in hand.

"Well, that much is obvious, or you wouldn't be here. It should have been obvious to my sister too. She's limited herself, relying solely on herbs. It has made her weak and now her coven is paying the price." Angelique rose from her perch with the grace of a panther.

The witch's graceful stride and long, full skirted dress gave the appearance that she floated across the room. She stood in front of the fireplace and warmed her hands over the crackling fire.

"She can't expect to fight something otherworldly with earth magic." Angelique tsked. "My sister should know better."

"But *you* can, right? You have the magic to fight the curse and make a cure for Marguerite's coven?" I hoped the subtle appeal to the strength of her powers would be enough to sway her to help us.

"Of course, I can." Angelique turned her back on the fire and faced me, meeting my gaze. "But it will cost you."

Galen and I had expected as much. Witches loved to barter. Magic wasn't free. With Marguerite, it had been an even exchange: shelter on pack lands for wards surrounding the property.

But I had a sinking suspicion, nestled in the pit of my stomach, that neither Galen nor I would be able to afford what Angelique was selling.

THIRTEEN

GALEN

Angelique was Marguerite's sister. I hadn't seen that one coming. The fact that Marguerite hadn't shared that piece of information with me before sending Talia and I out for a cure shouldn't have surprised me. That woman played things close to her chest.

Something I related to as alpha. I didn't share any more than I had to with pack outsiders. Still, a heads up about what Talia and I were walking into—on her behalf—would have been nice.

The witches in my town preferred to blend in with the community. Here, the witches *were* the community and the town operated as a front for their coven. They used glamours to conceal their presence and limited their contact with the outside world.

The less people who knew about their dark magic practices, the better. They were less likely to be arrested that way. Humans were fine with the supernatural until things got messy—and dark magic was definitely messy.

"Tell me, alpha, are you willing to pay the price for the cure to save my sister and her coven?" Angelique opened an ornate metal box on the mantel, retrieved a cigarillo, and proceeded to smoke it, flicking her ashes into the fire.

"It depends on how much you're asking." I was pretty sure she wasn't going to ask for cash, but I could hope. I did have some money stashed away for emergencies. I figured a demon curse qualified as an emergency.

"No, that's not how this works. It's a yes or no question." Angelique took a long drag off the small cigar and blew a smoke ring in my face.

"I like to know what I'm buying." I folded my arms over my chest and held my ground. I wasn't agreeing to anything without the details first.

"You know what you're buying. You're buying a cure for the demon afflict—"

"And how much I'm paying for it," I interjected, since she seemed hell bent on splitting hairs.

"You're either willing to pay it or you're not." Angelique turned her attention from me to Talia and my stomach clenched up in knots.

Talia had already sacrificed enough. She had a demon mark. I wouldn't let her take on a debt for Marguerite when the witch couldn't offer anything in repayment. She'd already said removing the mark was beyond her.

Talia didn't need to owe anyone anything.

"What about you, little wolf? I see you're willing to make deals with demons." Angelique pointed her cigarillo stub at Talia's wrist. "What about with a dark witch?"

"I didn't make a deal with a demon." Talia jutted her chin and squared her shoulders. "The demon marked me, but I never asked for or received anything in exchange."

"You're telling the truth." Angelique's eyes widened as she flicked the rest of her tiny cigar into the fire. "That is very unusual. A demon doesn't mark a wolf for no reason."

"I'll pay it," I growled, drawing the witch's attention away from Talia.

"Excellent." The witch clasped her hands together and stepped away from the fireplace, the flames flaring behind her. "Your first-born for the cure to the demon curse."

"What?" Talia's hands curled into fists at her side.

I hadn't given children much thought since Jessie died. I hadn't seen a future with anyone else.

Until I met Talia. She made me want things I hadn't in a very long time—including a family. Love. Commitment. Children.

"Oh, your faces." Angelique swept her long blond hair to one side and draped it over her shoulder. "I'm just kidding."

Talia didn't relax her hands. If anything, she looked even more upset than I was.

"No one's laughing." I moved to put myself between Talia and the witch.

As much as Angelique needed to be knocked down a peg, we needed the cure she had to offer.

"So serious." Angelique rolled her eyes and sighed. "Fine, fine. We'll just get down to business then. The terms of this agreement are final and binding."

She ran through the legalese of a contract that bound us to the terms of the exchange. Terms we hadn't negotiated because all sales were final and sealed in blood.

Sacrifices had to be made.

Angelique revealed a small athame hidden in the folds of her skirt. She ran the blade over the pad of her thumb and sliced it open. Blood welled to the surface and ran down the back of her thumb, across her palm, and down onto the carpet.

"I, Angelique Lilith Marchand, high priestess of the Noctum coven, offer this potion and the knowledge of my foremothers needed to imbue it, to Galen, alpha of the Long Claw pack." She slid the blade back into the folds of her skirt and clicked her fingers, a scroll appearing out of nowhere. Then she swiped her thumb across a leathery scroll and marked it with a swath of her blood.

I wasn't sure what the parchment was made out of, but it wasn't rags or wood pulp. I decided it was best not to think too hard on it. Otherwise, I might lose the nerve to touch it.

"You haven't said what you're asking in exchange for the cure," I said.

"Well, since you so rudely refused my first offer..." Angelique's mouth curved into a devilish grin. "I'll take a marker to be called in at a later date of my choosing."

"A marker?" Talia seemed confused by the witch's request. "Is that like a favor?"

"Yes, that's exactly what it is." I pinched the bridge of my nose and closed my eyes. "A favor for her to call in whenever she wants."

"At my beck and call." Angelique dangled the scroll in front of her. "Your name in blood is all that's required to seal the deal, alpha."

"What kind of favor?" Talia leaned forward. She narrowed her eyes into slits as she examined the document's fine print.

"Anything, really." Angelique yanked the document back, rolled it up, and held it behind her back. "But if those terms aren't satisfactory to you and your... *friend*, another offer has just come to mind."

"I think you should hear what the other offer is before you decide, Galen." Talia wrung her hands together. "A favor to her could literally be anything. It's better to know ahead of time what you'll be giving up."

I wasn't thrilled at the idea of owing Angelique a favor either, but I had a gnawing suspicion that whatever her payment up front was, it would be worse than the lay-away.

"What's the other option?"

"I'm glad you asked, alpha." Angelique's ruby lips peeled back in a wide smile that revealed sharp incisors, no doubt filed to a point on purpose, and a small black crystal embedded on each side along the gumline. "Your seed."

Man, I hate being right.

"Think about it." The witch sighed like a well-satiated lover. "A half-witch, half-wolf child. The blood of a high priestess and alpha running through her veins. She would be magnificent, a force of nature."

"*No!*" Talia's answer on my behalf was like a gunshot going off in the room.

She wasn't my mate, but she'd just laid a claim in front of Angelique.

"Does she do all the talking for you?" Angelique pulled the scroll out from behind her back and ran it down my chest. "According to the lunar cycle, it is the ideal time for creation and conception. One night of your life, Galen Long Claw, for the lives of many."

"You're asking for more than one night. That's a lifetime commitment." I ignored the pointed stare Talia gave me for putting that much consideration into the offer.

Angelique hadn't been kidding about the firstborn. We'd just assumed the worst and she had some sadistic ritual in mind. But what she really wanted was a child.

She'd been steering me toward a coupling from the moment I'd asked for the cure.

Her eyes turned sultry as she said, "I'm in need of a donor, not a co-parent."

Father a child, then abandon it? *I don't think so.*

Talia was growling, low in her chest, as if her wolf was about to rise up and break free.

"I'll take my chances with the marker." I snatched the scroll out of her hand, bit down on the tip on my index finger hard enough to draw blood, and scrawled my name across the bottom of the contract.

Talia's sigh of relief pierced the awkward tension building between me and Angelique.

The witch pouted. "More's the pity."

The scroll retracted with a snap of Angelique's fingers and disappeared into thin air. "Aubrey, bring the potion."

Aubrey waltzed into the room balancing a silver tray on the flat of her hand. She rotated her arm and extended the serving tray to

Angelique. In the center of the tray was a liter-sized clay jar with a cork stopper. A paper tag dangled from twine cording wrapped around the neck of the bottle.

"As we agreed." Angelique removed the potion from the tray, checked the tag, and handed the bottle to me. "One cure for the demon curse. My sister will know what to do with it, but I've included detailed instructions in case she has any questions."

"Thank you, Angelique." I passed the jar off to Talia and extended a hand to the high priestess.

"Don't thank me yet, wolf. Save your gratitude for when I call in my marker."

Angelique's laughter followed us out of the parlor, into the foyer, and onto the front porch.

"Galen." Talia stopped midstride and clutched my arm. "What's to stop Angelique from using her marker for... for her hybrid child?"

"Nothing, I'm afraid." I turned and cupped her worried face in my hands. "I'm not the only alpha around. She has her fair share to choose from. We just have to hope that when the time comes for her to call it in, there's something she needs even more."

It wasn't much, but it was the only consolation I had to offer her.

The marker was a blank check for Angelique to cash whenever she wanted. It was possible all I'd done was delay the inevitable. Still, I had the cure, and the witch was without child. And Talia's wolf had settled back down behind her beautiful eyes. I had to take that as a win.

"Let's get going while the getting is good." Talia cradled the jar to her chest, leapt off the front porch, and rushed down the sidewalk out on to the street. It was like she couldn't wait to put distance between us and Angelique.

I was hot on her heels.

Aubrey didn't see fit to grace us with her presence to escort us back to the coffee shop where we'd left my truck. Talia and I retraced our steps through the alleyway. Instead of cutting through the coffee shop, we followed the alley out to the end, banked a right at the corner building, and hauled ass down the sidewalk back to the coffee shop.

"If I never come back to this place, it will be too soon." Talia was buckled up in the passenger seat the second I unlocked the door.

At least one of us had the option never to return.

I climbed behind the wheel, threw the truck into reverse, and tore out of town.

We reached the main gate on the pack's property an hour and a half later. Marguerite and Sarah were waiting for us on the edge of the coven's encampment. Both were eager to have the cure in their hands so they could replicate and administer the potion to their witches.

"You might have warned us about Angelique." Talia thrust the clay jar into Marguerite's hands.

"It was imperative you went in with a clear mind, free of influence from me. Had she sensed my influence in relation to your opinion, she may not have helped us." Marguerite checked the tag hanging from the neck of the bottle.

"I don't think she was helping us at all," Talia grumbled. "She helped herself."

"My sister only ever does anything if she stands to gain from it." Marguerite handed the cure over to Sarah with instructions to place it by her cauldron and wait for her before she began the replication process. "What was the price?"

"A baby." I pinned her to the spot with a stern gaze.

It was a good thing she had given the clay jar to Sarah, otherwise she might have dropped it on the ground and lost her one chance at saving her coven.

Her hands clutched at her throat. "You didn't promise her one?" Marguerite's concern over her sister's desperation for motherhood confirmed my choice to roll the dice with a marker instead.

"Not quite. My options were to impregnate her tonight or agree to an undisclosed favor to be called in at a date of her choosing."

"We can only hope and pray to the goddess that she finds herself in need of something else from you in the future." Marguerite lowered her hands in front of her and bowed. "My coven and I are in your debt, Galen. The price for our salvation was higher than I anticipated and for that I am truly sorry."

Her contrition did a lot to soothe the jagged worries in my soul. "Just take care of your coven, Marguerite, and finish the wards surrounding the property as soon as you're able."

My phone buzzed in my back pocket. I recognized the pattern of the vibration for the silent ringtone. It was the one I'd assigned to my father's number.

"I need to take this call." Phone to my ear, I excused myself and stepped outside. "Hey, Dad. How are you feeling?"

"I've felt better, son." His voice was thready and weak.

The illness had ravaged his body, but up until then, his spirit had remained strong. He didn't sound like himself, and I feared I was losing him. "I'm coming, Dad."

I hung up and popped my head back into the tent. "Talia, I have to go."

She'd grown fond of the old man in the time she had been staying with him, and she took as good, if not better, care of him than I did. She prepared his meals, kept his room clean, but more importantly she kept him company.

"I'll come with you." She started for the entrance to the tent.

"It's been a long, strange day and there isn't an end in sight, so why don't you stay here?" I went back into the tent and pulled her into my arms, resting my chin on the top of her head and breathing her in. "We're both on the schedule for watch tonight, so I'll go check on my dad and be back here in an hour or so."

"We could really use another set of hands here, if you don't mind helping out, Talia?" Sarah zoomed by with an armful of ingredients, busy as she and her comrades were trying to replicate the cure.

"Okay, let him know I'll be in to check on him in the morning and give him a hug for me." Talia held on a little longer before letting me go.

I jumped in the truck and zoomed home. There, I slipped inside and sat next to my father's bed.

He'd deteriorated since I'd seen him last. The illness was working harder to take him away from me, and my father—our alpha, the strongest man I knew—was too tired and weak to fight it off any longer.

I was losing him.

This man was more than my father; he was my best friend and confidant. A sounding board when I needed advice, a shoulder to cry on. He'd raised me to be the man I was today. I owed him everything.

I sat in the chair beside his bed and filled him in on everything that had happened with the witches, the demons, and the pack. I spared him the detail that he'd almost been a grandfather. I wasn't sure his heart could take that little snippet.

I listened while he doled out more sage advice about my life. More specifically, my love life and Talia.

"She's the one, Galen." He gripped a pillow against his torso and coughed. "Marry her or I will. She won't refuse a dying man his last request. I'll steal her right out from under you."

"You think so, huh?"

"She lets me win at checkers. I'm telling you, she's as good as mine if you don't make a move." He rolled to his side and settled deeper under the covers. "Now, get out of here. I need my beauty sleep. I've got a hot date in the morning."

Our roles had reversed. It wasn't something I'd expected or prepared myself for. He had taken care of me all my life. It was my turn to do the same for him in his final days.

My heart hurt as I tucked him in the same way he used to tuck me in at night when I was a little boy, pulling the covers up over his shoulder, kissing his temple, and wishing him sweet dreams.

I wasn't ready to let him go. I doubted if I ever would be.

FOURTEEN

TALIA

I was worried about Max. Galen had left earlier to check in on his father and spend some quality time with him before he was due back for security detail. I'd hoped to get an update on how Max was doing but didn't want to intrude on their time together.

Galen would let me know how Max was, whenever he got back.

Until then, I had my hands full helping Sarah and Marguerite administer the cure to the afflicted witches.

They'd followed the instructions Angelique provided and brewed enough of the potion for each member of the coven to receive a dose. Some of the witches, most likely the first affected by the curse, needed a double dose.

Even Sarah took some, just to be on the safe side, even though her affliction seemed to have passed.

Marguerite started another batch while Sarah and I measured out the doses.

The two worst affected witches were still sedated and strapped down on cots in the makeshift infirmary. Sarah and I worked in tandem. She held their mouth open, and I poured the potion down their throat.

The second batch of the cure cooled in a cast iron cauldron on the table. Marguerite planned to administer any second doses needed herself once the potion was ready.

Sarah and I completed our rounds of the more stable, but still affected, witches. By the time we reached the last witch, our first patients were waking up. It was a huge relief to see them all coming back to good health.

Like shifter healing ability, there was something to be said for the healing properties of magic.

And for Angelique's recipe—though I'd never admit that to the dark witch. "This is amazing." Sarah took my tray of empty paper cups and set it on the long wooden table. "They're already so much better. Look at them."

"Do you think they remember what happened? What it felt like to be cursed?" The demon mark on my wrist itched again.

"I'm not sure, but Marguerite will no doubt have a lot of questions for them when she feels they're ready to answer them." Sarah's gaze traveled to my wrist, her mouth forming a little 'o' when she put two and two together on why I'd asked. "So the curse and your mark aren't the same type of demon magic."

"Demons have their own magic?"

That was news to me.

"It's not like ours." Sarah shrugged. "It means a lot to me that you're here, Talia. With everything you have going on, you took the time to help us. I won't forget that. Marguerite won't either."

"That's sweet, Sarah, but you're my friend. You don't owe me anything for helping people who need it."

Besides, the only thing I wanted, they couldn't give me.

I checked my phone for an update from Galen. Nothing. I supposed no news was good news.

It was almost time for my watch. I said my goodbyes to Sarah and Marguerite and headed over to the meeting house to check in with Markus. I was grateful for the time alone. The walk afforded me a much-needed opportunity to clear my head. So much had happened recently, all of it strange.

Especially our trip to Jarrettsville.

Angelique had freaked me out, mostly because of her request for a hybrid baby with Galen. My wolf had almost jumped out and forced me to shift right there and then on the spot.

No way was that woman—*any* woman—getting her hands on my man.

My man? I couldn't help but feel proprietary over Galen. My feelings for him were growing stronger by the day and the thought of him spending intimate time with someone else had instantly gutted me.

I had hoped to get information about my mark during the visit, but hadn't gotten anywhere. It was obvious she knew something about it but uncovering what she knew would likely come at too high a price.

They weren't the only dark coven out there. I would find my cure and get the demon mark removed one way or another.

The moon hung low and heavy in the sky. There weren't too many shadows thanks to the moonbeams illuminating the path, but I couldn't shake the feeling that something was lurking in the darkness beyond the tree line.

I decided to investigate, following my intuition to the spot where I'd sensed someone watching me, but there wasn't anyone there.

Damn, Talia. You're really freaking yourself out. Knock it off.

I started back for the path.

A crunch came from farther back in the woods. It was like Natasha all over again. Someone was out there, most likely waiting to attack. Which meant, it was likely one of the Northwood pack members.

"There you are." My old alpha leaped out from the cover of the trees. "I was beginning to think you weren't going to show up tonight."

My blood boiled at the sight of the man who'd murdered my father. "What are you doing here?" I spat the question at him.

"Looking for you, obviously." He leered, exposing his canine teeth. "It's no surprise I would find you prowling around. Just like your mother used to."

"My mother?" It was the first time I'd heard anyone say anything about my mother in years.

My father had always hated talking about her. It hurt him too much.

"Like mother, like daughter. She was a whore too. Ask your father. Oh wait, you can't. I killed him. You'll just have to take my word for it." His vitriolic words and acidic laughter shattered the peace of the night.

I glared at him, feeling my wolf rise up ready for the call to shift. "My mother wasn't a whore, and neither am I."

I was still a virgin. Not that I was about to tell him that, but calling me a whore was the last insult I'd take personally.

"Maybe not. But she was just as dark, just as tainted as you. That mark on your wrist is proof enough. She wasn't sure if your father was really your father. Did you know that? He was too stupid to care and married her anyway." He stalked forward, closing the distance between us.

I inhaled sharply, clenching my hands into fists. "You're baiting me into a fight and I'm not going to fall for it."

As much as I wanted to beat his ass into next month, Galen had drafted papers to formally challenge him. I'd promised to respect the process.

Of course, that had been before the Northwood pack alpha showed up on pack land, looking for me and spewing all kinds of hateful bullshit.

Galen couldn't blame me for defending myself if this asshole attacked me first.

I couldn't hide the smile that crept across my face. I hoped he would attack. Then I could beat the system and have vengeance without going back on my word to Galen.

I just needed to play this stupid wolf's game and get him to hit me.

Piece of cake.

"You didn't waste any time moving on to the next wolf. How long did you wait after your breakup with my son to jump into bed with Galen?" The alpha spat at the ground beside my foot. "Power hungry bitch. Your mother was the same way. Fucking every wolf she could just to get ahead in the pack. You don't believe me? I'm speaking from experience, sweetheart."

Vomit. Gross. No way.

"You're talking a whole bunch of bullshit is what you're doing." I kept him talking, trying to make him mad enough to take a swing. "No one cares what you have to say, especially not me. It's why you're hemorrhaging wolves. You can't keep your own pack together."

His lip lifted in a snarl. "Ha, the wolves who left are useless creatures anyway. My pack is better off without people like you or that worthless girl Natasha." He circled around me, stalking his "prey".

Only, I wasn't his prey. He just didn't know it yet. My plan was working and it wouldn't be long before he struck.

Like a villain in a movie, he kept monologuing. "I suppose you think you're clever. Trading up from my son to Galen. After all, Maddox won't become alpha for decades, but Max will be dead in days."

I bit down hard on my lip to stop myself from screaming out at him. *Bastard.*

The alpha kept going. "But it won't last. He'll see you for what you are soon enough and when he does, you'll be tossed out of another pack. Assuming you live beyond tonight."

He lunged without warning, fist raised, in a superman punch maneuver. His fist slammed into my chin. My lower jawbone cracked and shifted out of alignment.

I staggered sideways, groaning at the pain splintering through my head. But I used it to focus. He'd drawn first blood, which meant it was game on.

I'd watched him fight off challengers enough times to know all of his moves. When he came at me with a left hook, I was ready, blocking it with my right and landing a looping left to his temple.

I caught him off guard and made the most of the opportunity by throwing another punch. And another.

He shifted his hands and swiped at my midsection with razor sharp claws, shredding my shirt. I ran my hand over my stomach, expecting to feel gashes and come away with blood on my fingers, but the only thing he'd slashed was cotton fabric.

The demon mark on my wrist pulsed. I felt a rush of energy unlike anything I'd ever experienced before. Was it giving me extra power?

"You made the biggest mistake of your life coming here, old man," I said through my clenched teeth and fractured jaw. The bones had begun to set crooked. I would have to have it rebroken for it to heal properly.

"A mistake? Hardly. I tried to rid my pack of the darkness. It started festering inside your mother when she was pregnant with you. And then you were born, and I knew it was inside you too. I could see it, smell it on you." He let his hands go in a flurry of punches.

I dodged most of his strikes, copping one solid punch to my ribs that knocked the wind out of me.

When I got my footing, I wheezed in a breath. "If you hated me so much, why did you let Maddox and I get engaged?"

I didn't understand why he felt the way he did about me. I wasn't a dark or evil person. I'd been an upstanding and loyal wolf in the Northwood pack.

None of this situation made any sense.

"My stupid son gets an itch he can't scratch, and you think that meant I endorsed your engagement? Please. Whatever evil you got in you, girl, is what lured him in. Poisoned my son until you had your way with him."

He swung again, but I dipped left and dodged the blow.

I tapped into the burst of energy from my demon mark and threw a series of devastating blows to his face, each one hitting their mark. My knuckles screamed with pain, but the effect was satisfying. His nose broke, his eyebrow split open, and blood poured down his face.

Galen's wolves howled in the distance. The cavalry was coming.

But for once, I didn't want back up.

I wanted to take out this bastard myself, and make him pay for what he did to my father.

To me.

To my mother's memory.

I hit him again. And again.

Markus was behind me, shouting something, but the words were a garbled blur. I was lost to my rage and the pulse of power from the demon's mark on my wrist.

By the time Theo and Markus reached me, my former alpha was a beaten, bloody mess. He was curled up in the fetal position, begging for me to stop hitting him.

The only thing that stopped me from killing him was the knowledge that I would have then been in the running to fill the alpha position for the Northwood pack. I had zero interest in ever being a part of that pack again. I kicked him once more in the ribs for good measure.

Galen wanted to challenge him, and he was welcome to officially unseat the alpha. I didn't see any reason to merge the two packs.

Except maybe Nyssa and Celia.

The memories of my old friends softened my heart, pushing the red haze further into the back of my mind.

"Talia, are you oaky?" Theo grabbed me by the shoulders and spun me around.

Markus checked the defeated alpha. Satisfied that he wasn't dying from his injuries and would live to attack another day, Markus ordered him off the property.

The Northwood alpha turned and hobbled back through the woods.

Asshole.

"Why does this stuff always happen when you're on watch?" Theo joked and poked me in the ribs.

"Ow." I gripped my jaw. "Don't make me laugh—it hurts. Don't make me talk either. That hurts really bad too."

"Let me take a look at you." Markus came over and examined my jaw. "It needs to be realigned. If we don't set it tonight, your bite will be off."

Theo offered me his hand to squeeze while Markus reset my jaw. White-hot pain spiderwebbed across my face and settled behind my eyes. My knees threatened to give out, but the two of them kept me on my feet.

"Galen needs to know what happened. Do you want me to call him for you?" Markus rubbed soothing circles in the center of my back.

I nodded. As much as I wanted to talk to him, the pain and swelling in my mouth limited my ability to talk. I needed a few minutes to recover and then shift to finish the healing process.

"Hey, are you okay? I just heard what happened." Darius jogged up the path, ignoring the others as he rushed to my side.

"I'm fine." I pressed my hands on either side of my face, supporting my jaw so I could respond.

The sooner I answered, the sooner Darius would leave.

Or at least that was what I hoped.

I wasn't sure how he'd heard about the attack so soon. The only other wolves on watch were Markus and Theo, and I hadn't seen anyone else when I left the witches.

So, who told him?

"Why don't I take you up to the meeting house? There are still a few cots left in there from the craziness with the witches." Darius gently squeezed my shoulder before trailing his fingers down my arm and reaching for my hand.

I shook my head and pulled away from his grip. I didn't want to go anywhere with Darius. He totally creeped me out. Big time. I needed to go with my gut and trust my instincts.

If I had done that earlier, I probably wouldn't have gotten kidnapped.

Oddly, that scenario worked out for the best. Still, that was a fluke situation and Darius was nothing like Galen. That nagging voice in the back of my head assured me that if I went anywhere with Darius, the situation would not have a happy ending.

Markus and Theo had Galen on a speaker call. They were both preoccupied with answering the multitude of questions he fired at them in rapid succession and hadn't seen my signal for one of them to intervene.

"Are you sure?" Darius asked in soft dulcet tones, the way one might speak to a child. "You need to rest, Talia. Just relax and let me take care of you."

He reached for me again, but I stepped back out of his reach. This time Theo caught the uncomfortable interaction.

"Talia, Galen wants to hear your voice. Even if it's a little garbled right now." Theo waved me over, inviting me to join in on their call and providing me an escape route.

I'd bested my old alpha in a fight and I was shaking from the relief. I felt confident I could take Darius if I had to, but so far, he hadn't done anything that warranted it.

He was weird and set off all sorts of internal alarms for me, but that was about it. I couldn't justify punching him in the face when all he'd done was offer assistance.

Darius had ingratiated himself into the pack. He'd spent time making friends and alliances, while I'd been busy running from one disaster to the next and leaving a trail of damage in my wake. The best thing I could do for the time being was to politely turn him down and avoid him whenever possible.

But if Darius started something, I wouldn't be afraid to finish it.

FIFTEEN

TALIA

Galen was on his way. Markus, Theo, and I all tried to convince him to stay with his father. The threat was over and there was no need for him to rush to me and miss out on time with Max.

He didn't listen.

He wanted to check the boundaries himself, meet with Marguerite for an update on the witches' recovery and work out a timeframe for the completion of the new wards.

And check up on me.

He was not convinced when I told him on the phone that I was fine. May have had something to do with my broken jaw that hadn't healed at the time of our conversation.

In this particular case, he was probably correct, and Galen may have had cause to worry. I was an effed-up, insecure, neurotic, and emotional mess.

My altercation with my old alpha had made me feel strong. But five minutes after he'd left, and my jaw was hurting like the blazes, the tears began to run. I shifted into my wolf form to help with healing, but also so I could hide from the pain inside of me.

The tipping point for my breakdown had begun.

I didn't want to be coddled and told everything was going to be all right. Because the mark on my wrist said otherwise. I wanted to be alone. There was so much rattling around inside my head I needed to process it all, and I couldn't do that with Galen or one of his betas hovering over me.

The pain in my jaw subsided as soon as the shift happened and would be one hundred percent better when I shifted back from four legs to two. Our ability to heal serious injuries was just one of the perks of being a shifter.

Speed was another.

I cut across the property, zigzagging through the trees, kicking up clumps of dirt and grass whenever I took a hard turn.

The crisp, clean air, along with the smell of fresh pine and even the decomposition of foliage on the forest floor, soothed the voices in my head.

But it didn't shut them up entirely.

The alpha of the Northwood pack's voice remained loud and clear inside my mind. He'd used a two-pronged attack—mental and physical. I'd heal the physical injuries easily, but the mental would take more than a shift to fix the damage.

He'd accused my mother of being a power-hungry gold digger and alluded to having an affair with her at some point. The thought of his hands on my mom disgusted me.

Worse than that, he accused her of being tainted by darkness. Of being evil. As if she were to blame for whatever plagued the pack.

He was a revolting man and unworthy of the title alpha. It was time for him to be dethroned.

He'd accused me of being just like my mother, not wasting any time moving up the ranks after my break-up with Maddox.

My relationship with Galen was still complicated, but I was in love with him, that was for sure. Our connection wasn't because I pushed him or manipulated our feelings. My new life was none of the alpha's concern, or anyone else's for that matter.

After all, he'd kicked me out of the Northwood pack and forced his son to end our engagement. He even made Maddox attack the Long Claw pack and me.

Just like he sent Natasha after me.

I'd earned my happiness and I was going to enjoy every second of it. Just as soon as I got rid of the demon mark on my arm.

All of my dark thoughts were like a storm cloud that hovered over my head and blocked out the sun.

I should be happy. The Northwood alpha had attacked, and I had defeated him. I'd beaten him. Not Markus or Theo. Not Galen. I did it on my own.

After years of living under his thumb, after the death of my father and my life being destroyed, I'd stood my ground. And I'd won.

It wasn't quite the vengeance I wanted, but it was a victory, nonetheless.

So why did his words hold such power over me? Why was every single negative thing he said ringing in my ears?

Running wasn't having the usual restorative effects on my mood, but I pushed harder and ran faster in the hopes that I would feel better. I wondered if Sarah or Marguerite had a potion that could cure the melancholy that had settled into my heart and mind.

Something, anything, to wash away the hurt and anger.

I ran the length of the boundary and cut across open ground at top speed through the field. The smell of my former alpha's blood lingered in the air.

His words continued to haunt me.

What had my father or I ever done to become the focus of his ire? He'd killed my dad because of a mistake, then tossed me aside like I was nothing.

The alpha had said he wanted to cleanse the darkness from his pack. He'd tried with my mother and then again with me.

I didn't understand what he meant.

Had my mother passed something down to me? Why hadn't my father ever said anything about it?

I always thought I was a good person. Had I been fooling myself?

Did he know something about me, and my family, that I didn't? I found it hard to believe that he would be privy to the Linetti family secrets while I'd been left in the dark.

That mark is proof enough.

The alpha knew I'd been marked. What else did he know?

The demon's symbol on my limb flared to life. It throbbed in time with the beat of my heart and seemed to grow stronger whenever I was angry or upset.

As if it fed off those darker thoughts and feelings.

The demon was feeding off me, eating my emotions.

The connection with the demon terrified me and I was frustrated that we hadn't made any progress in getting the mark removed.

The longer it stayed on my arm, the deeper the demon's claws sank into my skin. The demon had a hold on me, had laid claim to my soul. It was just a matter of time before it came to collect.

Part of me wished it would.

At least then the waiting would be over. All the uncertainty was wearing me down. I was always putting on a brave face while everyone else's emergencies took precedent and the most pressing matter in my life was put on the back burner once again.

If the demon would only come for me, then I could at least fight him and try to win my freedom. To prove that the darkness wasn't really a part of me. At the very least, I could attempt to find out his name.

But the demon never made a move.

Its pieces were all on the checker board, safely in the back row, while I was forced to wait for it make a play and advance across the board.

Galen called my name, but I couldn't face him. I'd gone to the dark corners of my mind, and I wasn't ready to come back to the light.

Not yet anyway.

I continued to run. Dirt packed in between the pads of my paws and in the grooves of my claws. Bits of grass and leaves clung to my coarse coat. I must have begun to look like a wild and feral beast.

In some ways, I was.

In the Northwood pack, I'd followed the rules, did what was expected of me, and never spoke up. I'd played the part assigned to me by Maddox and his father.

But I wasn't that wolf anymore. In truth, I never had been. I'd made myself smaller to fit inside the box they'd put me in.

A box that turned out to be a cage.

I'd thought I loved Maddox and worse, I'd thought he loved me. But Maddox didn't know what love was any more than I did.

We were both wrong. It wasn't love at all.

But maybe he and his father were right about one thing. I was moving on too fast, clinging to Galen and the safety net he provided. Not because of a desire for power but for security.

But is it really too fast when the whole world is crashing down and coming to an end?

Demons were running lose, cursing witches, killing humans, and attacking wolves. The town was destroyed, and the people looked to the pack to fix it. But the packs were at war with each other, and dark witches might have been the reason behind all of it.

When I thought about everything that had happened since Galen made the fateful mistake of kidnapping me with the hopes of gaining an advantage over the Northwood pack, my feelings didn't seem rushed at all.

It felt like I knew exactly what I was doing. At least where Galen was concerned.

The rest of it, well, I was making it up as I went along. There wasn't really a precedent for demon marks outside of a barter.

Galen was intentionally loud, lumbering around in the woods, stepping on branches or piles of dead leaves to make his presence known. He stayed close, following my every move, but never invaded my space.

He respected my need to be alone and at least tried to give me some semblance of that. It went against his better judgment as an alpha and as my kind-of-sort-of-maybe boyfriend. I knew that he wanted to keep me safe.

But I wasn't sure that he could.

Not if what the Northwood alpha had said was true.

How could Galen keep me safe from myself?

We continued like that, with me running and Galen following. He never pushed. He just waited, giving me the space I needed to work out everything on my own.

He was a patient wolf.

The story of how we met was an unorthodox one, but it was ours and I was grateful he had crashed into my life.

Galen filled the cracks of my broken heart and mended it back together. He showed me a true partner didn't expect you to lessen yourself but built you up and helped you shine.

He showed me what real love was.

And now I was running from him.

I reached the lake and padded out to the end of the dock. The placid black water looked like glass in the moonlight. I smacked my paw against the surface and watched the ripples spread out, distorting my reflection.

The tiny wave I'd created dispersed, and the mirror finish of the lake's surface returned.

I hardly recognized the wolf staring back at me when I peered down over the edge of the dock. The pointed ears, long snout and black nose, and the thick, dark gray fur coat were all mine and familiar.

But the eyes belonged to someone else.

The intense sapphire blue eyes I normally boasted in my wolf form were gone. They'd been replaced with fiery red orbs. An unnatural, unholy color that belonged on a demon and not a wolf.

Terror gripped my heart.

What is happening to me?

I smacked the water again with my paw, destroying the reflection, and waited for the surface to calm once more, willing the image to be different.

The same wolf stared back at me—red eyes and all.

I gave voice to my fears and howled at the moon.

Was I all those things that the Northwood alpha said I was? A vessel for the darkness. Wicked. Evil. Damned.

The proof seemed to be staring me right in the face.

Was this how a demon was able to mark me without being summoned or a deal being struck? It sensed some sort of evil inside me and claimed it for itself?

Like recognized like.

Galen answered my call with a howl of his own. He must have sensed my distress and decided enough was enough.

He prowled out of the tree line and approached the dock.

Panic set in. *He can't see me like this. If he sees my red eyes, he'll freak out.*

I couldn't bear to see the fear or disgust in his eyes when he saw me like this. It would shatter my already fragile heart.

"Talia?" Galen shifted back to human form and charged down the dock. "What's wrong?"

I prayed to all the gods in the universe that my eyes would return to normal when I shifted.

Please, please let them be normal.

When I was human again, I gripped the edge of the dock and peered over into the water. The red glow was gone, and I was back to myself.

Whatever it was that had caused my eyes to turn a hellish shade of red seemed to only affect my wolf. At least that bought me some precious time. It was still a problem, but one I could work with short term.

As long as I didn't shift around any of the other wolves, and that included Galen, the problem could be contained. I could search for an answer. It had to be connected to the demon mark.

My best chance at finding a solution to the mark and glowing eyes lay with a dark witch.

One darker than Angelique.

Still, she was a starting point. I'd sworn I would never go back to Jarrettsville, but I needed help. Help I couldn't get anywhere else.

Angelique's knowledge and power came at a price. One I hoped I could afford. And yet, what choice did I have? I would have to pay whatever it cost, to fix this.

"Are you okay?" Galen knelt down beside me, the flat of his hand caressing the small of my back. "Talia, talk to me. Tell me what happened, please."

I did the only thing I could.

I lied.

THE END

The story continues in Wolf of Thorns:
https://books2read.com/wolf-of-thorns